"I'm glad I met you today, Danny."

He looked right into her and felt heat spear through him. Never had he known anything quite as right as this. It was as though he'd found something he hadn't been aware he was searching for. "Back at you, Brooke."

She seemed to be considering something as she sipped her drink. Then, she stretched up and placed a light, whiskey-flavored kiss on his mouth. All the while her eyes never left his.

The heat flared, spread like wild fire throughout his system. The last of the tension unleashed inside, pressing into his gut, his groin and—dare he admit it—his heart. Surely not. His hand trembled, sloshing his drink to the rim of the glass. Putting it down, he reached for her. "Brooke, can I kiss you? Properly?"

Her glass joined his before her breasts pressed into his chest and her arms reached around his neck. Her lips met his. "Yes," she whispered between them. "Yes, please."

Dear Reader,

Six months ago, a massive storm hit the Marlborough region, and especially the Marlborough Sounds where I live. The damage was huge and repairs to roads and properties are still ongoing. My husband didn't arrive home from work and it took hours to find him as the phones were out, but he was safe and dry. People lost homes, including a family who'd only moved into their new home six days before.

When I started Brooke and Danny's story, I just had to use this disaster as the background. Being cut off from everything we take for granted had different effects for different people. Brooke and Danny had never met before, and yet they were quick to get together to help a trapped neighbor. They were quick to get together in other ways, too. But Danny has a lot of issues to deal with and he's not so sure Brooke will see them as he does. But he can't walk away from her. She's his heart's desire.

I hope you enjoy their story and how love wins over everything.

Sue

suemackayauthor@gmail.com

STRANDED WITH THE PARAMEDIC

SUE MACKAY

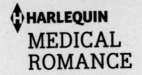

HARLEQUIN
MEDICAL
ROMANCE

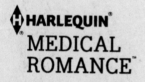

HARLEQUIN®
MEDICAL ROMANCE™

Recycling programs for this product may not exist in your area.

ISBN-13: 978-1-335-73742-7

Stranded with the Paramedic

Harlequin Enterprises ULC
22 Adelaide St. West, 41st Floor
Toronto, Ontario M5H 4E3, Canada
www.Harlequin.com

Printed in U.S.A.

Sue MacKay lives with her husband in New Zealand's beautiful Marlborough Sounds, with the water on her doorstep and the birds and the trees at her back door. It is the perfect setting to indulge her passions of entertaining friends by cooking them sumptuous meals, drinking fabulous wine, going for hill walks or kayaking around the bay—and, of course, writing stories.

Books by Sue MacKay

Harlequin Medical Romance

Queenstown Search & Rescue

Captivated by Her Runaway Doc
A Single Dad to Rescue Her
From Best Friend to I Do?

London Hospital Midwives

A Fling to Steal Her Heart

Reclaiming Her Army Doc Husband
The Nurse's Secret
The GP's Secret Baby Wish
Their Second Chance in ER
Fling with Her Long-Lost Surgeon

Visit the Author Profile page
at Harlequin.com for more titles.

For all our friends who helped each other
throughout the storm that decimated our area.
It has been quite a ride.

CHAPTER ONE

'HEY, BROOKE. I don't know when, or if, I'll get to join you. But it won't be today. The ferries are cancelled, and there're no flights into Blenheim either. Add to that, Wellington Airport's on an extreme weather alert.'

'No surprises there.' Brooke shivered as the gale slammed into the house, almost as if it knew it was being talked about. 'This weather is unbelievable,' she told her sister. 'I'm amazed we're even having this conversation. I had no power or cell phone coverage for most of the night. It came back on ten minutes before you rang.'

'The weather app looks as though it's going to get a whole lot worse yet. You stay safe, you hear?'

Saskia was wearing her big sis hat, the one that said, *I'm always here for you, Brooke.*

As she was for Saskia. 'Not a lot I can do about anything. The rain's torrential, and the house shakes with every blow. The wind's like nothing I've known, and that's saying something.' Having spent her childhood in Wellington, the world's supposedly windiest city, she was used to gales, but this one was something else. 'Seriously, sometimes I think the house is going to take to the sky.'

'Jeez, Brooke, I don't like the thought of you dealing with that on your own. Wish I was with you.'

'No, you don't. You'd be changing your knickers every five minutes.' Brooke managed to laugh even as the large bay window overlooking the storm-tossed sea sounded as though it was about to implode. So much for taking a relaxing break from her hectic job over in Nelson where she worked as an advanced paramedic.

Saskia laughed. 'True. I am such a scaredy-cat when it comes to storms.'

Brooke was meant to be having a week with her sister, lazing around catching up on what they'd both been up to over the past few months. Brooke sighed. As much as she was comfortable with her own company, she'd been looking forward to spending time with Saskia. They never shut up when they got together, always had plenty to say. Her sister was one of the few people in her life who hadn't tried to make her do things their way. She and their dad. Saskia never came up with nasty surprises like their mother used to do such as 'You're changing schools today'. It might have been because she was being bullied, but some warning would have made the change less stressful and given her time to get used to the idea.

Like the morning when she awoke to be told she wasn't playing with her friends. Instead, she had an appointment with the dentist to have six teeth removed because they were growing wrong. No one had mentioned there was a problem when she'd first gone to the dentist with her mother. The *surprises* didn't stop there. Not all so drastic, but each one undermining her confidence and taking away her right to face her own problems. Their mother used to say it was her way of protecting her girls from unnecessary worry. Eventually, as she grew older, Brooke understood where her mother was coming from, but her mother couldn't accept that was not how she liked to face these things. She preferred to be prepared.

Her ex had been no better. In fact he had been worse, surprising her with shocks such as 'I've found somewhere better to rent and we're moving on Friday. You'll have to take time off work to pack up the house.' There had been another instance when he'd flipped her life overnight, and by then she'd had enough so she had packed her bags for the last time and left him. She should have done it sooner but in her book loving someone meant accepting them for who they were, even if it meant giving up some of her own dreams. Up to a point, and she'd reached that point then. It seemed she was always having to stand up for herself. Even her first boyfriend used to hide what he was up to from her, not telling her he intended going offshore as soon as he qualified as a doctor until one day she overheard him talking about it to another medical student. No wonder she found trusting people difficult.

Saskia cut through her memories. 'Who else is in the bay that you could spend the night with?'

'I'm fine, really.' Who was she trying to convince? It was a little creepy sitting here, listening to the weather beating down on the house so fiercely, hearing the boards groan and the roof creak. But there was nothing she could do about it. She'd cope without knocking on doors for a bit of company. She had a pile of books to read, and the fire was cosy.

Plus, she was still having much-needed time out from work. This break was essential for her sanity. The weather wasn't wrecking that, although the beach walks looked as though they were off the menu at the moment as well as the talking she and Saskia would have done. Recently, along with a shortage of qualified paramedics, there'd been an abundance of patients with severe injuries that had tested her skills to the limit. A couple hadn't been saved, which got her down at times. It didn't always pay to be too caring. Would she have been happier to still be working in a laboratory sitting behind a microscope and not having to front up to people while dealing with their health issues? No way.

Strange how she'd always liked the idea of working in the medical world, and because she'd loved science at school and always got top grades she'd thought being a lab technician would be the ideal career. The problem was that she loved being involved with people and the lab just wasn't right for her. Test tubes and microscopes were kind of dull, even though the work was fascinating. After working as a volunteer ambulance officer in her spare time Brooke had quickly known where she wanted to be, and had become a full-time crew member on the ambulances, advancing up to an advanced paramedic in little time. It seemed she'd found her niche—hands-on helping people was a perfect fit.

'You still there, Brooke?'

'Yeah.' Miles away. 'The only lights I saw before we lost power during the night was next door in Mike and Paula's place, and a car there I don't recognise. It was bucketing down when I got up an hour ago, so I haven't gone to check to see if Lloyd's here. I'll go shortly. I presume he's tucked up inside.' Old Man Duggan had lived in the bay since well before their parents bought the small, basic beach house next door to him thirty-odd years ago and it was a family thing to always knock on his door whenever they came here for a break.

'It's not like he'd have his lights on,' Saskia said. The old man went to bed when the sun went down, summer and winter.

'It was spooky not being able to see what was going on in the dark,' Brooke admitted. There were no such things as streetlights out in the Sounds so the only light at night was from the stars and moon, which were notable by their absence due to the dense cloud coverage.

'Stay in contact,' her sister said. 'We know what major slips have done to that road before. They're saying this is a one in one hundred years storm.'

The only road giving access to the area cut along the edge of the hills rising above the sea and didn't always remain in place when bad weather struck, bringing landslides spilling across the road.

'Don't panic if you don't hear from me. It's more than likely there'll be other power outages before this is over.'

Right then the lights flickered.

Brooke held her breath.

Flick, flick.

The light settled, became constant again.

'Talk about tempting fate.' Outages had happened all too often in the past for her to think today would be any different. Besides, if this storm was battering the rest of Marlborough, the power company would be crazy busy.

'What happened?'

'Power nearly went off. Right, the gas bottle's going to need changing soon so I'd better go get the spare from the shed. I'm not looking forward to getting blown about and saturated to the skin.' It looked a bit spooky out there too. While it was daytime, outside was dark as dusk. 'Talk later, if we can.'

Placing her phone alongside the lantern she'd put out along with matches last night, ready in case of problems, Brooke got the shed key, slipped into gumboots and a rain jacket and headed out into the maelstrom. *Should've done this when I first arrived yesterday*, she thought as a gust shoved her sideways. So much for being prepared for the worst-case scenario, something they'd been taught as kids by their father. Unlike their mum, he always prepared them for the worst, which was something their parents never agreed about, thereby causing a bit of friction at times, their mother thinking they should just get out there and enjoy themselves without worrying about anything. Dad believed staying at the beach might be all about having fun but remembering that things could go wrong when the weather decided to flick from good to bad was equally important. Saskia was Brooke's opposite; she always avoided problems until they could no longer be ignored. But she still supported Brooke in her decision to face up to those same problems.

When she'd arrived last night the wind had seemed to be abating, so she hadn't worried about getting the gas bottle. Instead, wanting to keep warm throughout the night, she'd replenished the firewood inside the house from the stack by the garage, then called it quits, needing food more than anything else, having missed lunch. Within hours of that decision, the storm had picked up to become more ferocious than she'd believed possible.

All around the property and in the neighbours' places, trees groaned and creaked as though their branches were about to fly off.

Small branches and twigs were scattered across lawns, snagged in fences and hanging from washing lines. Water poured down from the hills, and a small torrent cut through the lawn where she was headed. It reached her ankles when she tried to stride across what was usually firm ground. The soil sucked her feet downwards. It was unbelievable. She shivered, tucked her arms around her waist and, head down, pushed on.

The ground felt as though it was moving, but that had to be her imagination. How could it move? It was the water, wind and rain making this feel foreign, nothing like the place she'd known all her life and spent wonderful summer holidays lying on the grass in the sun, wearing a bikini and working on getting a tan.

Splat. Brooke landed on her backside in mud. Great. Shoving upright, she took more tentative steps towards the shed in the back corner of the property. Her feet went from under her. This time she landed on her side, her thigh taking the brunt of the impact. How come it was such a hard landing when water and mud were supposedly soft? On all fours, she pushed up and back onto her feet. Did she really need the gas bottle so badly? If the storm went on for much longer then yes, she did. What had she been thinking, not doing this last night when it would have been easier? And safer. She shivered. This was no picnic.

Slowly, one step at a time, she finally made it to the shed.

'Hey there. Are you all right?' A male voice reached her during a brief lull in the wind.

It wasn't a voice she recognised. The owner of the car at Mike's? 'I'm fine. Getting a gas bottle. Do you need something?' she yelled back.

'Just checking up on people,' came the shouted reply.

That was nice of him, whoever he was. He certainly wasn't a regular, she knew them all, so he must be staying next door. Moving away from the shed to go around to the side door, her feet once more shot out from under her. This time she managed to keep her balance. 'I am so over this,' she groaned. She'd be turning black and blue all over.

'Wait there. I'm coming to help.'

'I'm fine,' she muttered, saving her energy for crossing to the door. Then she swore. The key was no longer in her grasp. Which fall had she lost it in? Looking over the ground she'd skidded over, she couldn't see the yellow plastic tag holding the key. 'Where is it?'

She tried the door in case someone had forgotten to lock it. Yeah, well, that was wishful thinking. Rule number one: whenever leaving the beach house make sure everything's locked. So, back the way she'd come, head down, this time scanning the mud and lawn. It was going to be a longer fifty metres than it had been on the way over.

Deep rumbling made her pause and look around. What was that? The ground seemed to shake. An earthquake? In the middle of all this? No way. That would be nature having much too big a laugh. But mud *was* rushing at her, pouring around her feet, up to her ankles, while her chest was thudding hard. Storms were bearable, but earthquakes were her nightmare. The lack of control and fear of what damage could be caused always turned her into a blithering idiot during one of those. But there hadn't been an earthquake. It was the storm dealing more blows she had no control over.

Crack, bang, smash.

The kowhai tree next to the shed bent towards her, a large branch snapping off as though it were a twig, hitting the ground hard, sending water and mud in all directions, a lot of it over Brooke as she tried frantically to get out of the way of the rest of the tree. Too late. The trunk landed beside her, branches entangling her legs and dragging her down into the muddy water, taking her down the sloping lawn towards the usually quiet creek that was now more like a river. She swore as her body tensed. This was ridiculous. She'd been taken down by a tree and if the noise was anything to go by there was more trouble coming. She needed to get away from here. *Yeah, right.* Like her feet were helping. Or her legs with their shaky muscles.

Get a grip.

'Hey.' That voice again. 'I'm here.' Then he swore. Must be catching.

At least she wasn't alone, which made her feel infinitesimally happier. If she was in trouble, far nicer to be there with someone else. Even a stranger was preferable to being alone. She might have toughened up when it came to men but nature could still undermine her resolve to cope with anything that was thrown her way. There was just no fighting nature, no winning against storms or quakes or seas that could devour a person in an instant.

Weird how she was moving, out of control, being pushed further down the lawn by the sheer volume of water and mud and getting closer to that torrent that was normally a small creek. It only ended up in one place—the sea—where thunderous waves were pounding the shore. Something wound around her arm, pulled against the flow. Something strong and determined to keep her from disappearing further down the way. Something soft yet firm. Human.

'I've got you.' A man. 'Try digging your feet in to get a purchase on the ground.'

Easy said when everything was so slippery. Was she going to get out of this at all? Safely?

'You can do it.'

The deep male voice beside her ear gave her confidence, something she hadn't realised she'd lost in the last few scary seconds. Brooke shoved one foot hard against the slithering ground, gained some purchase. Then she shoved even harder with the other and felt a brief shot of relief as that too dug in deep. Pushing upward, she came upright against the man saving her from sliding further down what had only minutes ago been an overgrown lawn. When she tried to pull a foot free to take a step, her foot came out of her boot. 'Great.' She reached down to tug the gumboot out of the mire. No easy feat, but eventually it was swinging from her hand.

'Let's go carefully. We'll do this together. Put your arm around my waist and hold on tight. I've got you.' The guy's voice was deep and edgy, but he seemed to know what he was doing.

Which made her relax further. She wasn't in this mess on her own, not that it was danger-ous now, mostly annoying. Then she looked around her and shuddered. It could become bad very quickly, the way the water was stream-ing down the hillside. She'd seen the results of heavy rain in this area before and wasn't silly enough to believe a massive landslide couldn't happen here.

'Right.'

Let's do this.

She placed her arm around him and began the laborious job of getting out of the mud, one squelching step at a time.

Whoever he was, Brooke wasn't worried that she was about to be abducted so he could have his wicked way with her once they were free of the mud. For starters, she'd belt him around the head if he even so much as looked as if he might try. Right now, she was more interested in getting onto safer ground. She'd find out who he was later.

'We need to go the other way.' Her house was in front of them. There was a new river running between her family's house and Old Man Duggan's. 'I want to go check on my neighbour, make sure he's all right.'

'Let's wait until this torrent is done with wreaking havoc all over the show. I'd hate to be caught in a further rush of water, or mud and trees,' her rescuer said as he turned them back towards her place.

He mightn't be from around here but apparently he was more aware of what was going on than her, because she hadn't noticed other trees now bouncing down the slope.

'Good call.'

'I thought so.' He sounded almost light-hearted. Almost. Some tension was underlying his words, and definitely in the arm gripping her close to his body. Then he slipped, and she was going down with him as his arm held onto her.

Digging her feet in hard, she tried not to topple. 'I've got you,' she repeated his earlier words.

He barked a sharp laugh as he struggled not to fall flat on his face. 'Yeah, right. Think I weigh a load more than you.' His feet did a couple of quick slides but he remained upright. 'Thanks. This is getting ridiculous.'

'Come on. A few more steps and we'll be out of the worst.' The unscathed part of the lawn was close, unless there was something she wasn't seeing in the whirling leaves and pieces of bark being thrown around by the wind.

'You're right.' Her companion pulled her

along, hell-bent on getting free of the mud. Sensible man.

Suddenly they were standing on terra firma, not being sucked into the mess that used to be a tidy grass yard. 'Thanks for coming to help me out of that,' she said. 'To think when I arrived here yesterday I thought I'd mow the lawns when the rain let up today.'

'Chance would be a fine thing. It's going to take a digger to clear away all the debris.'

'As far as I know, there isn't one anywhere near here. A guy has one in a bay further along the road, but he'll probably be busy clearing storm damage there once the rain and wind stop.' Brooke began crossing to the house. 'Let's get out of this.'

On the porch she shrugged out of her coat and hung it on a peg by the door. Relieved to be safe, she turned to the man who'd helped her and tensed. He was drop-dead gorgeous. Even when covered in mud splatters and with his sopping-wet hair flattened on his skull, he was—stunning. Lifting her arm, she was about to wipe a splodge of gunk from his cheek, but realised just in time how stupid that would have been. He was a stranger. She did not touch strangers—except in her work, trying to help someone. So what was it about this man that had her wanting to run her hand over his face? It must be a reaction to the last few minutes, worrying about getting back to the house in one piece.

Taking a step back, she tried for normal, which was hard to do when her heart was suddenly beating as if a wayward drummer had taken over. 'I'm Brooke Williams. Are you staying in the cottage next door?'

He nodded. 'My name's Danny. I came a couple of days ago with Paula and Mike. They went back to Blenheim yesterday morning, and I'm staying to enjoy the quiet for another couple of days. Except—' He gave a wistful glance over the yard. 'Nothing quiet about this.' There was a definite Aussie twang going on in his voice.

'You're not the only one hoping for some relaxation. We were going to have some quiet time. My sister was meant to come over from Wellington, but that's not happening any time soon.'

Too much info, Brooke. You don't know this man.

But he had come to help her and didn't look evil.

'I wouldn't want to be crossing the Cook Strait in a plane or ferry. It'd be diabolical at the moment.'

'Everything's cancelled. You said you were

checking up on people. Who else is staying in the bay?'

'As far as I could ascertain, only the man in that house beyond yours. I was coming this way when I saw you heading across to your shed. Thought you must've needed something important to be out in the weather so figured I might be able to give you a hand.'

'That was kind. I had intended getting the spare gas bottle but must've dropped the shed key when I slipped.' The remaining boot wasn't coming off easily. It was moulded around her foot. Using the top of the step as leverage, she pulled hard and finally it shot off, sucking at her foot as it went.

'Is there a spare key? I could get the tank for you.'

'Thanks, there is, but I'll make do in the meantime.' She'd go light on using the stove top. 'You'd only get into the same trouble I did.' She mightn't be so good at hauling him out of the mud as he'd been with her. Now she had time to really look him over there was a lot standing before her. At least two metres tall, she reckoned. Her head barely reached his shoulder. Hard to see his outline with the heavy wet weather gear he wore, but he didn't appear to be carrying excess weight. More fit and muscular, if what she'd felt when he had his arm around her holding her tight was anything to go by. 'I still want to check up on Lloyd though.'

'Let's see what happens over the next hour. The weather might clear a bit and the water running off the hill might slow some, then we can tackle getting to the house and possibly your shed.' His mouth was sexy when he smiled. There was a cheeky twinkle in his eyes now they were out of the rain and safe from the sliding mud. 'So you're on your own?'

Forget sexy or beating heart or good-looking. 'I think I'll go inside now. Thank you once again.' She put her hand on the doorknob, ready to go in and lock him out. She didn't feel vulnerable, but she also wasn't stupid enough to take any risks. He was a stranger, and if that smile was anything to go by, a right charmer when he put his mind to it. There were other people in bays along the road if she had concerns, but it wouldn't be easy getting around at the moment. Attracting someone's attention if she needed to would be near impossible, especially with the likelihood of phones not working.

'Hey, I'm sorry if that sounded bad. I was merely thinking that you might prefer to join me rather than see this out alone.' He stepped off the porch onto the path. 'I only had your safety and comfort in mind.' Danny sounded genuine. What was more, he looked it.

Brooke felt awful for doubting him. Kicking her boot aside, she said, 'It's me who should be apologising.' She needed to accept not all people came with hidden agendas. 'I'm used to hanging out here on my own. My parents own this place, and my sister and I also like to spend time here together for catch-ups whenever our busy lives give us a break,' she said in a bid to be friendly. 'We've been coming here since we were toddlers.'

Talking too much now, Brooke. He doesn't need your life history.

'What I'm saying is I'm fine on my own.'

CHAPTER TWO

DANNY BREATHED DEEP, exhaled slowly. For one worrying moment there, when Brooke went all stiff and tight on him, he'd thought she'd recognised him. But she hadn't, had only been responding to his offer of company, and he'd overreacted. Nothing new in that. He did it so often, it was a habit. One meant to save him a lot of aggro or harassment, but which didn't always come out right. Come to think of it, she'd looked cross, not about to hug him and try to become his instant best friend. That made him happy.

'I'll head back to the cottage then.' Where he could breathe easier. Not get sidetracked by an interesting woman who might, for once, not want anything to do with him other than what he had to offer today. Company and help if required.

One of the best things about this working trip to New Zealand was that not as many people recognised him as in Australia and he could occasionally move around uninhibited by overzealous fans wanting to offer commiserations about his failed, once stellar and rising career as a professional golfer. It was great being able to go where he liked without ducking out of the way of eager individuals wanting to talk to him, especially females who wanted to be joined at the hip with the offer of the hottest sex he'd ever get, supposing he'd fall in love and not let them out of his sight. Unlike at home in Oz, in this country he could breathe a little freer and be himself—a medical intern—and enjoy everything that came his way without looking for hidden agendas. Except he was always on his guard, because the times he relaxed were when he got caught out. He had been busted in Blenheim, but for some reason the fuss had died down fast. A small town with lots going on and no time for outsiders maybe? Who knew, but he'd been happy.

Brooke seemed to be wanting to make up for her blunder because she started talking again before he'd made it off the deck. 'Hopefully there'll be access out of the bay soon after this weather bomb has finished. The road gangs are usually quick to clear the road enough for the many people relying on it for getting to work or going to doctors, getting groceries, you name it, to be able to get out.'

'Good to hear. I'll need to leave on Monday.' How long was this gorgeous woman staying? She'd said her sister was meant to join her so surely they'd planned on a few days here? Now that the sister mightn't be able to get through for those few days, Brooke's plans might change, whatever they were. Crazy, but he'd like to spend a little time with her, get to know her some.

Which was so out of the blue it made his stomach squeeze. He had no idea why he felt that way. His usual practice was to avoid getting close to anyone other than mates and family. She'd rattled him with that sudden sharp look when he'd asked if she was alone. As if she was on alert, but he sensed she was also quite capable of looking out for herself. The hint of wariness shifting through her expression suggested she had seen another side to men she did not like.

'I'll leave you to it. But I'm serious about going with you to check on the neighbour.'

Her smile was brief. 'I'll be fine.' With that, she stepped inside and shut the door without another look his way.

Danny shook his head, grinning stupidly. This was getting better by the minute. He was so not used to people doing that. Brooke didn't know who he was and, even better, didn't appear to want to know. It had been a very long time since he'd been ignored, and he loved it. Plodding through the sodden long grass to the house he was staying in, a trickle of amazement—even excitement—heated his groin.

Settle, man. This can't last.

His secret was so well known, eventually someone would let her know who he was, even here in New Zealand. But wouldn't it be great to let loose for a change? Have some fun with a gorgeous woman for once? There'd been a couple of looks from her suggesting she was sizing him up. Was she contemplating the same thing? Fun out here where they were alone with no one to spoil it for him would be amazing. And who knew what might come of a few minutes of relaxed conversation with a lovely-looking woman? In a couple of days he'd be out of here, on his way to Nelson and work, while who knew where Brooke would be? There wouldn't be any follow-up to a brief tryst even if she was single and happy.

He was so damned cautious these days it made for loneliness and longing for what there was to take if only he could lighten up. Not easy when most women he'd dated and thought he could get to know well and possibly fall for were more interested in his fame and money than in Danny himself. Brooke wasn't rushing to get to know him. Which was exactly why his blood was heating.

Talk about getting ahead of himself. Which only went to show how long it had been since he was seriously involved with a woman. The ones who dropped in and out of his life these days weren't welcome to hang around. They always wanted something he wasn't prepared to give. They believed they'd be the one to change his mind about getting into a permanent relationship. Nearly every woman he'd dated in the past six years had thought that and had wanted him to accept they were right for him, that they'd be the one to turn his life around.

The one exception had been refreshing. At first Brenda had been unaware of his background and accepted him as he appeared to be. He'd met her when he did a spell at an outback medical centre, and they'd had a fantastic few weeks together—then the time had come for him to return to med school in Melbourne and she had followed to spend some time in his territory, so to speak. Within hours she'd learned the truth and greed filled her eyes. She had started demanding more of him, a house in the most expensive area of Melbourne, trips overseas, clothes to die for. It wasn't happening. He had a medical degree to finish, followed by specialising in radiology. Then there was the way Brenda had changed so fast, her love no longer about the man she'd met in the outback and all about what he could bring her. He was out, done with her. Another layer of hurt added to his problems. It had been hard enough dealing with losing his career at a time when it was going stellar without adding the way he was treated by women.

So far he hadn't found that woman who'd take him on for who he was these days, the man who'd put his golf clubs away and hunkered down to study medicine. He'd love to find a woman who was more interested in all the characteristics that made him who he'd become. Not only in the man who'd earned a small fortune playing professional golf before the incident that killed his career, but a guy with dreams to be a doctor, a husband, a father.

Leaping into a pool to save the son of a world-renowned businessman from drowning had made him even more well known around the globe. He'd smashed his shoulder and all the ribs on one side of his body when he'd hit a concrete bollard he hadn't seen in the pool. The shoulder had never been the same. It was the end of golf. The end of a lot of things. But the boy had survived, and for that he was grateful.

Maybe if that had finished the media following him everywhere he went things might have turned out differently, but he was still loved so much for his fame rather than who he wanted to be. Not being seen for everything he was wasn't good. It made him feel he wasn't loved for the right reasons.

Danny made his way up to the deck of the tidy little beach house—Kiwis called them bachs, he reminded himself—and kicked off his boots. His gaze cruised over to the next-door property. Being stuck here might prove interesting. *If* that meant catching up with Brooke Williams again. It wasn't as though he had much to do now that the other two had gone back to town. Spending time with Brooke and having a chat about anything that came to mind was the best option to fill in his days he could come up with. That could be fun, and he'd be careful, wouldn't push himself into her space, but he was here if she needed help with anything.

Crack.

A loud sound broke through the bay.

Crack, crack.

'What the—?' Danny froze to the spot.

Whoosh. Bang, Thud.

Rushing water tore down the hillside beyond Brooke's house. Right at the spot where he'd helped her. Mud followed. Then rocks, a boulder and trees were heading towards the neighbouring house. This was getting out of hand.

Bang. Slam. Crash.

'That's too close for comfort,' he muttered. 'Forget close.' The house had taken a slam dunk. Boots back on, Danny began running towards the flooding between that house and Brooke's.

Brooke appeared on her back step, shoving her arms into her wet weather jacket as she charged down the step and onto the lawn, her focus entirely on her neighbour's house.

'Be careful,' he shouted. 'Everything's moving fast.'

'I need to get Lloyd out. If he's there.' She didn't waste time looking his way or slowing to let him catch up. She was on a mission.

So was he. Keeping her safe was paramount. 'Brooke, slow down. Carefully does it.'

She was slogging through the mud that had previously trapped her, but this time it wasn't holding her back. The determination in the set of her jaw said it all. She was going to the other house come hell or high water. Both of which they were already dealing with.

He caught up with her and grabbed her arm. 'Take it slowly. Falling and injuring yourself won't help your neighbour.'

Crack.

More rocks pelted down in front of them, banging into the building. 'This is way serious.'

Brooke stopped abruptly, looked all around and back to him, worry blinking out of those hazel eyes. 'You're right. What was I thinking?' She tugged her arm free of his hand. 'Not one of my brightest moments.'

'You're concerned for your neighbour.' Something he'd appreciate if he was in a dire situation, especially coming from this woman. Water was pouring through the shed door, which had been slammed back on its hinges. Mud and debris were also heading inside. The wooden structure groaned as a boulder slammed into the wall and widened the doorway.

Danny grabbed Brooke's arm again as she started ploughing through the mud. 'We're doing this together. We need to keep an eye on what's coming down that hill. Getting knocked off our feet by more mud or even a boulder won't end well.' That was putting it mildly. One of those rocks could kill anyone in its path.

She jerked her arm free and stared at him. 'You think I'm stupid?'

Well, she had been charging across without

taking any notice of what was happening before he'd intervened.

It must've dawned on her what she'd said because she suddenly laughed, and it was a surprisingly light, sweet sound that touched him tenderly. 'Yep, I'm stupid. Come on, let's get to Lloyd's before anything goes horribly wrong. I think I owe you a coffee when we've got a free moment.'

'Sounds good to me.' He'd prefer something stronger, but he wasn't saying.

She stomped through the mud as though that'd stop her getting stuck.

A deep rumbling sound ripped through the noisy air, tightening Danny's spine as he spun around to see what was happening now. 'Crikey.' He'd been wrong to slow her down. 'Run, Brooke.' He tried to get his feet moving but they were glued to the ground in mud, sucked down hard. 'Run!' he shouted. Brooke mustn't get caught in the landslide heading straight for them.

'Here.' She was tugging at his left ankle. 'Pull hard.'

Slurp. His foot came free. 'Get away from me, Brooke.'

She had his other ankle in her hands. 'Pull.'

Quicker to do so than argue. He hauled at his leg, pulling and pulling, then *bang*. His foot was out and he was sprawled on his back on the ground.

Brooke had her hands held out to him. 'Grab hold.' Her eyes were wild with fear as she looked up the yard. 'Most of it's going beyond us. But hurry.'

Shoving up, he reached for her hands and abruptly stood up, swaying with the intensity he'd risen. 'Go. Leave me. I'm fine.'

'Look out. Run.'

Danny didn't stop to look at what might be rushing at him, instead he did exactly as Brooke said. He ran. Slipping and sliding, gripping her hand, trying to keep them both upright. The woman beside him was all over the place. Every step she took became a skid in a different direction.

Then she went down.

And he was on his knees beside her, falling so his shoulder took the brunt. Bad move.

A tree rolled over them. The branches scratched at the skin on his face and hands. Then the trunk slammed into his ankle, bounced away.

'Jeez,' Brooke gasped. She was in the midst of smaller branches and stone-laden mud, scrambling to stand up. 'Danny? Danny, are you all right?'

His name sounded wonderful on her tongue. 'I'm good.'

How had she moved from the branches to right beside him so quickly when her legs were entwined with a wild passionfruit vine? 'Get away from here before something else comes down the hill,' he growled. 'Go on. Move.'

'I'm not going anywhere without you,' she snapped and reached for him with a grimace.

'Are you injured?'

'Just a few bruises. Nothing to worry about. What about you? Any damage?'

She was assessing him as though she knew what she was doing. Medically trained?

'I'm fine.' Above the wind he could hear groaning as outside boards popped off the framework of the house under the strain of the heavy layer of debris that had built up against the back wall.

'Crazy,' Brooke said as she approached. 'I've never seen anything as bad as this before.'

'Can't say I have either.'

'Lloyd's eighty-one, and while he's spry for his age, he's not going to come leaping out a window. I have concerns. Who knows what it's like inside? This will break his heart.'

'I'm coming in with you. I'm a doctor.'

'I'm an AP.'

An advanced paramedic. Then if Lloyd was

injured he was going to be in good hands. Brooke was probably a better option than him. She'd be used to major trauma on site without all the medical equipment that came with an emergency department, whereas he was a trainee doctor who usually only dealt with trauma after the patient had been brought into hospital.

'Right, let's do this.' She shuddered, then braced herself.

Crack.

A loud sound broke through the bay.

Crack, crack.

'What the—?' Danny froze to the spot.

Whoosh. Bang, Thud. Rushing water tore down the hillside right where they'd walked moments ago. More mud followed. Then rocks, a boulder and trees.

'Dangerous.'

Bang. Slam. Crash.

'Yes.' Brooke's curt reply made Danny smile. 'Definitely dangerous.' But she didn't move, as though afraid of what might happen if she went inside. Or of what she might find.

Danny gave her a gentle nudge. 'I'll go first.'

She shook her head. 'No. I can do this.'

'Then I'll be right behind you.'

'Thank you.' She shuddered, then braced

herself. 'I'm going in through the kitchen window. It's already broken.'

Danny nodded. Whichever one that was, the sooner they did this the better for all of them, especially the man inside. 'I'll give you a leg up once I've knocked out the remaining glass.'

'No need.' She was there, reaching inside, avoiding the sharp pointed pieces of glass still attached. 'I've got the latch.' With that, she pulled the window frame open. 'Amazing it's still straight. Thought it'd be out of whack after what's happened.'

'Is there another door that might open? That would be easier than trying to climb in through there.' Danny nodded at the window.

She stared at him. 'I'm a dope. Of course there is. Just around the corner, at the front, which might not be in good shape either.'

She was nothing like a dope, but he wasn't wasting time telling her, only to be rebuked. 'Worth checking out.' He was already on his way, followed by Brooke. 'Doesn't look too bad,' he said the moment he set eyes on the door. 'But we need to be careful after what's gone in through the back of the house.' He tried to open it. It didn't budge.

'Let me help.' Brooke came alongside him.

For an instant he breathed fruit. Light and sweet, and appetising. Her perfume? He couldn't think where else that intoxicating scent came from. Together they pushed into the panels with their shoulders. Nothing happened. 'We're wasting our time and energy. Back to plan A.'

Brooke stepped further along the front of the house.

'Hey, come back. That's not safe.'

'It's all right. I'm just grabbing this.' She lifted a wooden crate from the wonky deck. 'I can stand on it to get inside through the window.'

'I'll go in first. Then I can help you on the other side.'

'That's not necessary. Anyway, I know Lloyd. You don't.'

And apparently her pride was on the line, if the way her shoulders lifted a little and her eyes turned steely meant anything. 'Call out to him and see if you get a response.' He was still going in first. They had no idea what it was like inside, and he didn't want Brooke getting caught in there.

But she was ahead of him, stepping onto the crate she'd placed below the window and leaning in. 'Lloyd, it's Brooke. Can you hear me?'

'I'm in the kitchen.' The reply came loud and clear, though a little wobbly.

Shock? Or pain from an injury? Danny wondered. Likely a combination of the two.

'Are you all right? Can you make it through to the lounge, where I've got a window open?' Brooke called out.

'I'm stuck. There's a lot of mud in here and I'm on the floor. Think I've done in my leg and I banged my head when the microwave flew off the shelf.'

'We're coming in. The guy staying in Mike's place is with me. He's a doctor.'

Danny drew a deep breath. 'You're way more qualified than me. I'm still an intern.'

Her eyes widened. 'You started late in life?'

'At twenty-four.' That was all he was telling her. For now at least. Which was more than he told any woman he met who hadn't recognised him. Because then they wanted to know where he'd been before he started his medical studies and why hadn't he gone from school to university and a hundred other questions he wasn't keen on answering.

She blinked, smiled and started to clamber through the window space. 'Sometimes older students are more prepared for what lies ahead. From what I've seen, anyway.'

Her smile loosened some of his determination to remain aloof about his past, though not enough to spill the beans on the career he had begun his working life in. Or the accident that had killed that dream. Or the fame and fortune he'd earned in a very short time. Anyway, they didn't have time for deep and meaningful conversation at the moment.

'Know what you mean,' he blurted. Because he truly did. He studied and worked mostly with med students six years younger than him, and there was a lifetime in those years that had matured him well beyond them. He no longer looked at life as being there to do with as he chose. Now he trod carefully through the mixture of good and bad, the expectations that were doused by any number of obstacles and understood how easy it was to decimate a person's hopes and ambitions.

'Ouch.' Brooke had dropped into the room and slipped on the sodden carpet. Looking around, she grimaced, her eyes widening as the house seemed to shudder. Her shoulders tightened as she squeezed her arms close to her sides. 'I don't like this.'

Creaks and groans made Danny tense and at the same time drove him to hurry and rescue the old man lying in the kitchen. Who knew how long this house was going to stay upright? He climbed in to join Brooke, but she wasn't waiting around for him.

'Lloyd?' she called. 'Where are you? I can't see you.'

'There.' Danny pointed to a foot poking

through a broken cupboard as he joined her, trying to ignore the sounds suggesting there was more trouble to come.

'Sort of in the pantry,' came a terse reply from beyond the smashed bench. 'Be careful. I don't know how long that bench's going to stay upright. It's wobbling back and forth like nothing's anchoring it to the floor.'

'No surprise there,' Brooke muttered as she squeezed around the offending counter and bent down. 'Am I glad to see you.'

Danny concentrated on checking out the situation and the safety hazards. The kitchen was pretty much wiped out, cupboards askew or torn from the wall and tossed aside, and there was a load of mud covering every surface. He tensed, not liking being in there at all. It was dark and broken and not exactly still. From where he stood, Danny thought the dining area hadn't been damaged beyond water and mud on the floor. Stepping through the doorway, he saw the hall walls were warped yet the first room he peeked into, a bedroom, was all right.

'The damage seems random,' he told Brooke. 'I think the main damage has come from where that boulder struck in the centre, but we need to work fast at getting your friend out of here.' And them.

Her face was grim. 'I know. But it's not

going to be simple. Lloyd, your left ankle appears broken.' She glanced at Danny. 'He's taken a huge knock on the head and is bleeding profoundly. I think there might be other injuries too.'

'Yet he's coherent.'

'That'll change once shock sets in.'

'He's shivering hard. His clothes are sodden.' Danny crouched down beside her and surveyed the man before them. 'This isn't going to be fun, I'm sorry, but getting you out of here takes precedence over everything else.'

'Leave me here with Jean. Get out yourselves.' The man's voice was wobbly.

'Who's Jean?' Another person to save?

'His late wife.' Brooke sounded sad. 'He's not as coherent as I thought.'

'That crack over the head might've done some serious damage.' The man's age wouldn't be helping. Danny carefully felt the offending ankle. 'Definitely fractured. We'll strap it once we're out of here.'

'Going out via that window isn't feasible,' Brooke said as she wiped blood from Lloyd's face.

'I'll see what's holding the front door in place.' Danny stood up.

'Please be careful,' Brooke said quietly, giving him a quick glance. 'I don't want you tripping up too.'

'Same back at you,' he said as she moved around Lloyd to where his arm was caught under a pile of broken plates and bowls that must've poured off the pantry shelves. A loud noise that sounded like timber twisting reached them and her head shot around. 'Where's that?'

'Get Lloyd as ready as you can.' Danny found the front door. 'No wonder we couldn't open it.' There was mud and stones in a pile about half a metre deep against it. 'I'll work at shifting these. Fast.'

'There should be a coal shovel by the firebox.' She stepped around the decimated pantry and bent down. 'Here. Something's on our side.'

He reached for it. 'I'll do this. Stick with Lloyd.'

Digging deep, Danny worked hard and fast from the other side to move the pile blocking the door. Apart from the fact they needed out of here as soon as possible, Lloyd would be getting colder with every minute they took to free him. There wasn't a lot to him so there was every chance of hypothermia setting in, adding to his woes.

'How are we going to move Lloyd? I don't have a stretcher on hand.' Brooke gave him a tentative smile, as though worried he might think she was being flippant. She began scraping away mud with her hands.

'I'll piggyback him.' When her shapely eyebrows rose and her mouth twitched, he grinned. 'I know. But seriously, it's the only way I can think of. If we took this door off its hinges and loaded him on that it would be too heavy to carry across to your house.'

'It would also take a lot longer to get out of here.'

'You're onto it.' They were in this together, thinking along the same lines all the way.

'I doubt Lloyd weighs too much. He's always been lean, but now he's downright skinny.'

He hoped she was right. His right clavicle didn't take kindly to a lot of pressure since being broken in two places when his dive to save the kid had turned into a direct hit for him. It had never been the same since, and while swinging a golf club was still possible, he'd never returned to his peak game.

'Age does that to a person.'

Brooke stood up. 'I'll try moving the door.'

They'd cleared most of the debris. Danny reached for the handle and pulled firmly. The door ground hard across the floor but it did open. 'Not bad. Let's get our man out of here.'

Brooke looked around as more creaks came from the walls and ceiling. Shaking herself, she headed back to the kitchen. 'Lloyd, we're getting you out of here. Danny's going to carry you on his back.'

'Haven't done that since I was a kid.' The old man tried for a smile, but pain and worry dimmed it fast. He was staring around his broken home. 'I'm sorry, Jean. I'll be back as soon as I can.'

Danny swallowed hard. The poor old guy was tearing apart inside. 'Come on, the sooner we're out of here the better.'

Brooke nodded, understanding reflecting back at him. 'I hope so.'

Between them they got Lloyd standing on his good foot and then, with help from Brooke, Danny lifted him onto his back.

'I'm right beside you both,' Brooke said. 'In case you slip, Danny.' Her worry over what they were about to do was pouring off her.

'Going to catch us, are you?' He smiled at her.

'You're not going to fall.'

'You're right. I'm not.' He was going to be very careful so that he got Lloyd to safety, which meant Brooke would be safely out of here too. One firm step at a time, he reached the door and went out onto the deck. Down the two steps, across the lawn, through the mud and water, which had slowed considerably since he and Brooke had first approached the house. He slipped, felt Brooke's firm hand on his arm as he righted himself and moved forward. They were a team. Both knew instinctively what had to be done and got on with it. But he wouldn't relax until they were inside her house and Lloyd was lying down.

'The wind's abated somewhat,' Brooke said. 'Might be calm enough to get the rescue helicopter in.'

He hadn't thought that far ahead. 'I guess that's the only option. The sea's too rough for a boat to come in.' Waves were breaking on the beach, pounding the sand as though with a massive mallet. 'Do you know for sure the road is blocked?'

'No, and I could go along on the four-wheel bike to check it, but I can't imagine it's clear. Not after all that rain and wind. This won't be the only slip between here and Linkwater. Even if it was, the Queen Charlotte Drive will have slips for certain.'

No access to Blenheim and the hospital that way then. 'First we need phone coverage.'

'It was working earlier, and now that the wind's dropping hopefully it still is. Otherwise

I'll have to use the marine radio on Mike's boat and get them to organise a rescue.'

She had it all under control. He was liking Brooke more and more by the minute.

CHAPTER THREE

'POWER'S ON,' BROOKE told the men as Danny stepped through her back door in his sopping socks, still with Lloyd on his back. He'd insisted on getting his shoes off, which had been a mission. She'd pulled at them while he'd balanced precariously on one foot then the other. 'Bedroom this way.'

'Can we have a towel?' Danny asked as he followed her.

'No problem. I'll grab some of Dad's clothes too. Lloyd needs to get out of his wet gear.' She pulled back the bedcovers and helped lower Lloyd onto the bed, where Danny began removing the shirt from the shivering man. 'Be right back.'

'Where's Jean?' Lloyd groaned through blue lips. 'Is she safe?'

'Yes, Lloyd, she's safe.' Brooke sniffed. She wasn't going to cry. Not now, not in front of Lloyd. Or Danny. Jean had died four years ago and Lloyd had never got over losing her. But then who would when they'd shared a love like her neighbours had? Something she hadn't experienced. She'd loved Brad, but they hadn't been as connected as Lloyd and Jean. Not many couples were.

'Brooke?' Danny nudged her gently.

'Sorry.' Looking away from Lloyd, she focused on what was necessary. 'I'll get some scissors. Otherwise those trousers aren't coming off without causing added pain.'

'What's she's saying is I'm not to tug your pants over that ankle that's giving you grief,' Danny said to Lloyd, even when it wasn't likely the old man heard, which told her Danny was a compassionate man. He gave her a wink. 'Okay?'

'I'll be fine.' That wink caused a softening in her stomach. He appeared cheeky *and* confident, yet there was something intriguing about him she couldn't ignore. Every now and then caution seemed to slip across his face and he'd tense a little. What that was about was anyone's guess, and she wasn't about to try and figure it out. She had other, more important, things to do. Like supplying towels and dry clothes and getting Lloyd warm. Followed by calling 111.

'Here.' She placed towels and scissors on

the bedside table. 'I'll see if I can get through
to the emergency services. While I'm at it, I'll
get the first aid kit. By then you'll have Lloyd
ready to be checked over.'

A frown appeared on Danny's brow. 'What's
in the bag?'

She was an AP, remember.

'Most things we might need. Except no serious painkillers, only analgesics.'

He put his hand in his pocket and removed
a set of car keys. 'Front seat of my vehicle.
There's a bag with something stronger in it.'

Like any doctor she'd met, he obviously
went everywhere prepared for a medical event.
Like herself, though she didn't carry the serious drugs as that was not allowed.

'Back shortly.'

'Brooke,' Danny called after her. 'Go carefully. It's still dangerous out there.'

'I won't be anything else. I'll check the
phone's got coverage too.' If Lloyd's ankle was
busted then he should be taken to hospital, but
whether that was possible was another thing.

It was a lot easier going across to Mike's
house than it had been in the other direction,
with no slips or racing water to contend with,
and she quickly found Danny's small bag and
got her much larger kit from her car before
heading back inside.

In the bedroom, Danny was checking Lloyd's foot. 'Have you got something we can make a splint with? The ankle's fractured and I think so are some of the metatarsals.'

'Here. Use this.' Brooke pulled out a thick plastic sheet that could be wrapped around the ankle. 'Lloyd, I'm going to look at that wound on your head. I'll try not to hurt but let me know if it gets too much.'

'Where's Jean?'

'Do you know if he has any health problems we should be aware of? Does he take medication for anything?' Danny asked.

'I haven't a clue. He's never talked about prescriptions or the likes.' She pushed her sleeve up to reveal her watch and reached for Lloyd's wrist to find his pulse and began counting silently. If only she'd thought to find out, but she hadn't expected to be in this situation. The pulse was a little rapid, but that was more likely due to mental anguish and nothing to be concerned about. Despair was mingled with pain on his face.

Pulling her phone from her pocket, she sighed with relief. 'Three bars. That's not bad, even on a fine day.' One of the few downsides to staying out in the Sounds was poor internet coverage in many areas. Too many hills to interfere with it. 'We're going to get you out of here as soon as possible,' Brooke said to Lloyd, mentally crossing her fingers.

'I don't want to leave Jean.' His voice broke and tears dripped down the sides of his wrinkled face.

She gently wiped them away. 'She'd want you to get help.'

'Emergency service. Do you require Fire, Police or Ambulance?'

If only it were that straightforward.

'I have an eighty-one-year-old man who needs to be hospitalised. He has a head wound, fractured ankle and possible internal injuries, but we're in the Marlborough Sounds, where road access is probably unavailable due to the storm going on. I think sea access is also unfeasible, and I'm not sure about the rescue helicopter with the wind factor.'

'Are you medically trained?'

'I'm an advanced paramedic, not currently on duty.' She glanced at Danny. 'There's also a doctor here.'

'That's fine, just making sure you understand the man's condition. Is there somewhere close a chopper can land?'

That was the problem.

'No. They've used our front lawn before, but that's not a goer today. They'll have to lower the medic and a stretcher.'

The woman said, 'I'm putting you on hold while I talk to the helicopter rescue service. Don't hang up.'

'I won't.' Digging in a drawer, she found a pen and paper and began writing down Lloyd's scant details to go with him, including Brad's phone number which was in her father's notebook. He didn't keep it because he liked the man who'd screwed with his daughter's heart, but because he cared about his friend and neighbour. Could she leave it up to the hospital to phone Brad? She could, but she wouldn't be able to look herself in the eye. This was about Old Man Duggan, not his grandson.

'What's happening?' Danny asked.

'The operator's onto the chopper service. They'll know what's going on here and if the weather's safe enough to fly in.'

'They'll come from Nelson, won't they?'

'Most likely, unless they're too busy, then it's possible the service will send one across from Wellington if the wind's quietened over the strait.'

'That's a big if.' Danny smiled. He really did a lot of that. Was he used to getting his own way by doing so? Or was he just a genuinely nice guy? Instantly she relaxed a little. How did he do that to her with simple smiles? But they weren't simple. They came with under-

standing and thoughtfulness. Almost as if he
knew she liked having him on her side at the
moment. But then why wouldn't he? She hadn't
tried to push him out of the picture. So far he
didn't seem overly assertive, nor wanting to
please her all the time like some of the men
she'd recently dated. But she knew they didn't
tend to show their true colours immediately.

Her ex-fiancé, Brad, certainly hadn't. He'd
been accomplished at fooling her into believing everything he did was for them and with
her best interests at heart. He wouldn't explain
why he'd signed them up for a second house
before the contract for the sale of the first one
had gone through. When the sale had fallen
through they'd survived the threat of bank-
ruptcy by the skin of their teeth and a load of
luck. But their relationship hadn't. That was
when she'd left him. Brad was never going to
change. He acted impulsively, causing a lot of
harm along the way.

Like her first long-term boyfriend, who'd
been reticent about sharing his ambitions with
her. No wonder she didn't trust people to be
honest with her and why she now refused to
let any man take control of her. Except, by
avoiding those sorts of men, she'd found herself dating men who enjoyed her strengths and
wanted her to be in charge so they could go

along for the ride, being compliant with her dreams. That didn't make her happy either. Relationships were meant to be equal on all counts. Even the one with her mother, though nowadays they'd reached an understanding and got along a lot better.

She was happy being single. There was no one to disrupt her plans or decisions. Then it hit her. Brad. She did have to call him. Lloyd's family needed to be told what had happened. She'd wait until he'd been evacuated before she dealt with that devil.

Danny was talking, calming their patient. And her? 'I've never experienced wind like we've had these past twenty-four hours. I'm from Melbourne,' he added.

Then his mouth tightened, and his eyes became wary. He hadn't meant to tell her that. Why ever not? Millions of Aussies lived in that city.

Did he think she might recognise him from somewhere? Maybe in a previous life, she thought as the operator returned.

'Are you there?'

'Yes.'

'It's your lucky day. There's a chopper leaving Blenheim to return to Nelson so they're diverting to come to you. Can you give me details re the location?'

'I can do better than that. I have the GPS coordinates.' Something her father kept on his desk for this exact reason. Yes, he tended to be a pessimist, but sometimes it was just as well.

'Excellent. Fire away.'

Brooke read out the numbers and heaved a sigh of relief. Help was coming, and sooner than expected. She gave Danny the thumbs-up. 'Fifteen minutes tops, I reckon.' A smile spread throughout her, lifting some of the chill that had settled when she'd gone inside Lloyd's house. Things were looking up. And the man crouching at Lloyd's side was looking better by the minute, mud-splattered and all. If she didn't get wound up about him possibly being secretive. But they'd barely met so there hadn't been time to talk much about themselves. She'd move outside in preparation for the chopper—now.

Danny lifted his end of the stretcher Lloyd was strapped onto and they headed outside with the rescue doctor, keeping one eye on their patient and the other on the slippery ground. Brooke was calm at the other end of the stretcher. The ideal paramedic to have by your side in an emergency. How did she download afterwards? Go for a run? Talk to a friend? A partner? Pour a stiff drink?

Lloyd had started slipping in and out of consciousness minutes after they knew the helicopter was coming for him. Danny's heart squeezed for the old boy, who'd been upset about leaving his wife. What was it like to have a love like that? If only he could find it and learn the answer.

Briefly he studied the set shoulders and slim feminine frame in front of him. Not beautiful in the traditional way, but Brooke had an inner beauty that shone through even when she'd been trying not to freak out inside Lloyd's house with the boards creaking and groaning, sounding as if they were about to spring free and let the outside in further. His skin had lifted in bumps and the hairs on the back of his neck stood up. A similar reaction to Brooke's, if he'd read her correctly. She'd shivered and rubbed her arms a couple of times while peering around the space they were in. But she'd carried on checking over Lloyd as though she hadn't a care in the world other than making sure her neighbour was going to be all right. She was one cool woman—with a whole lot of apprehension going on in that trim body.

The medic was talking into his radio, presumably telling the paramedic still on board the chopper to lower the winch because Danny could see it beginning to drop from the side opening.

The downdraught from the rotors pelted them and flicked up water. No one bothered to talk. They wouldn't be heard above the racket the helicopter made. It didn't matter. The medic had everything under control and it was obvious Brooke had been in this situation before as she knew what was required, which was for them to continue holding the stretcher while the winch was attached. Within minutes Lloyd was on board and the medic was spinning in the air as he was lifted up to join his crew.

'See you around, Tristan.' Brooke had her hands around her mouth as she yelled at the swinging medic, who waved back.

Danny turned for the house, grabbing Brooke's hand on the way, leaning in to shout above the noise, 'Let's get out of this.'

She didn't even blink, just went along beside him, almost running, her shaky hand in his. So she wasn't as calm as he'd believed.

'It's been quite a morning, hasn't it?' he said when they charged up her steps.

Her boots went flying, followed by her jacket and then she was pushing the door open. 'Come in.'

Not the most enticing invitation he'd had,

but probably more genuine than any he could recall in a while. He could get used to this anonymity. Except—His heart lurched. It wasn't good to be dishonest and not saying who he was might be construed as that. Anyway, eventually the truth would out and moments like this would disappear once more.

'Yes or no?' Brooke stood there, hand on hip, a look of *What are you waiting for?* on her gut-stirring face.

His shoes hit the wooden deck with a clunk and his jacket joined hers on the wicker chair. 'That's a yes,' and he grinned. 'If you don't mind a bit more mud around the place.'

'Couldn't care less,' she said over her shapely shoulder as he followed her to the kitchen, where she went to stand in front of the firebox, rubbing her arms hard.

'Cold?' A chill was creeping into his body now that they were out of the wind and downdraught. He removed his damp jersey and moved beside her, stretching his hands out to the heat like she was.

'A bit.'

Another thing he liked about her was she didn't yabber on for the sake of it. Strange how that had him wanting to hear more from her.

'Is that why your hands are shaking?'

She stared at her hands, fingers splayed,

then turned them over, flexed her fingers. 'That and the tension finally easing off. Now Lloyd's safe and we're out of the way of any harm, it's all catching up.'

'It was scary in that house, with all the noise making me think the roof or walls were going to collapse in on us at any moment.'

Her eyes met his. 'Think I'd have preferred being at work dealing with a worst-case scenario than in there.'

He couldn't help himself. He took her hands in his and rubbed the backs with his thumbs. Her skin was freezing. 'You were great. I couldn't tell that you were so worried.'

Her hands tightened around his. 'Same back at you.' The tip of her tongue appeared between her lips. 'Thanks for helping me and Old Man Duggan.'

'No problem.' As if he wouldn't have. Even if she'd been falling over in her haste to get him to notice her he'd have done his darnedest to get her neighbour to safety. It was a bonus she hadn't acted in that way.

'It was heartbreaking, listening to him talk about Jean. Asking if she was safe.'

'It made me sad, and also thinking how much in love they must've been.'

'They were.' She nibbled her lip with a far-away look in her eyes. Then she straightened, once more appearing focused. 'Do you want a tea? Or coffee? Or something stronger?' She still hadn't pulled her hands away.

'I'll go for stronger if you don't mind. It might warm me up a bit more than tea.'

Her eyes were large and now filled with relief, not a hint of the wariness that had been there when he'd first left her on her back porch. The shaking in her hands was easing, and she'd moved ever so slightly closer. It would be effortless to wrap his arms around her and hold her close, sink his chin into that damp, dark blonde hair and absorb some of her strength and warmth. She'd kick him where it hurt if he did. Wouldn't she? He wasn't about to find out. It wasn't the way to get to know her better. He stepped back, pulling his hands free.

Disappointment met his gaze. Then she shook her head. 'What's your preferred drink?'

'Scotch, if you've got it.'

'Dad's favourite. And mine.' Then she grinned, as though a load had fallen away.

Danny felt as if everything was right in his world. Which had to be a first for a long time. 'Something else we seem to have in common.'

Her left eyebrow rose. 'Along with what?'

'We worked on Lloyd as though we've always worked together. We helped each other through the mud and water, got in and out of the wrecked house without any explanations required.'

'True, we did,' Brooke agreed.

'I take it you've been on other cases where the flying rescue service attended. You knew that medic.'

'Often. I work for the Nelson ambulance service.'

A gentle nudge in his gut. 'Another thing we share. I'm starting work at the Nelson ED this coming week.'

Brooke laughed as she crossed to a cupboard and poured two generous drinks. When she handed him a glass she tapped hers against it. 'Here we are, warming up in front of the fire, having a drink and admitting we got a little scared in there. I'm glad I met you today, Danny.'

He looked right into her, felt heat spear through him. Never had he known anything quite as right as this. It was as though he'd found something he hadn't been aware of searching for. 'Back at you, Brooke.'

She seemed to be considering something as she sipped her drink. Then she stretched up and placed a light, whisky-flavoured kiss on his mouth. All the while her eyes never left his.

The heat flared, spread like wildfire throughout his system. The last of the tension was unleashed inside, pressing into his gut, his groin and, dare he admit it, his heart. Surely not. His hand trembled, sloshing his drink to the rim of the glass. Putting it down, he reached for her. 'Brooke, can I kiss you? Properly?'

Her glass joined his before her breasts pressed into his chest and her arms reached around his neck. Her lips met his. 'Yes,' she whispered between them. 'Yes, please.'

She was to die for. All heat and tenderness and strength and giving and demanding. He devoured her with his kiss. And gave as good as he took. It wasn't enough. He should stop, but there were no brakes available. His body leaned further into her, bending to fit against her torso, to feel more of those exquisite breasts, her stomach, her hips and thighs up against him. It still wasn't enough. She made him feel safe. Safe from the danger of the storm. From the women who tried to tell him how to run his life and grab what they could for themselves along the way. He was safe from the world for a short while.

Don't ask him how it happened. Not even torture could make him answer the question, but next they were lying on the mat in front of the firebox, naked as the day they were born, and warm for the first time in hours. Hot, not warm. Heated beyond reason, need pouring through him as he reached to hold her tight, and to touch every inch of her skin, to feel her softness, her moistness.

Brooke wasn't lying still. She had an agenda of her own. Her hands were all over him, touching, rubbing, teasing, setting him further alight. Driving him insane with need. To the point he had to grab her hands to slow her down. She came first.

Nope. They came together. Both ready in such a hurry, impossible to ignore.

The conflagration was over almost before they'd started, and it was the best he'd known. Brooke was beyond any encounter he'd ever experienced.

Reluctantly he slid off her, but immediately took her in his arms as he lay on his side, breathing long, deep lungfuls of warm air as his heart rate slowly returned to normal. Under his hand he felt Brooke's heart rate slowing too. It was so cosy—and surprisingly intimate—lying on the mat with the fire's glow touching them. Especially since they hadn't met until a few hours ago. But *what* those hours *had* delivered. Could be this was the way to go—leap in and see where he landed? It had been quite the morning. Quite the introduction.

Long may this last. But it couldn't. He knew all too well how it would play out. Not necessarily today, or even tomorrow, but one day she would learn who he was. That was if they saw each other once they returned to their real lives in Nelson. What were the chances? He'd like to follow up and spend more time with her, which was bizarre in itself. He actually wanted to spend more time with Brooke, have more than a passing moment with her in front of her fire. Usually it was the other way round, and he'd be walking away.

Brooke ran her finger down his cheek. 'You're exactly what I needed.'

His gut tightened, and his heart lightened some. 'Know what you mean.' Except he thought he might need more of her, not less. Whatever had caused them to fall into each other's arms, share their bodies, it had been so good he felt relaxed in a way he'd forgotten was possible. That should be a warning, right there. This wonderful woman was doing things to him that he hadn't felt since he was an innocent nineteen-year-old heading up the chart towards number one for the under-twenties in international golf.

His girlfriend, Iris, had believed she was on that chart with him, and grabbed every opportunity to make a name for herself as his partner. That had been hard to deal with when she was back in Australia while he was playing around the world. He couldn't quieten her down, no matter how often he told her he wasn't interested in putting his whole life on the platform, only his golfing skills. Worse, she would often get a part in the interviews on TV whenever he was featured, either at his side or as an added feature. He'd loved her, but possibly not as much as he'd believed because his love had dried up the more demanding she became. She'd given up studying for a degree in accountancy because he was going to make a fortune and she'd be able to help him spend it. He suspected he hadn't listened hard enough to her earlier on in their relationship.

Then he had got it wrong again with Brenda. Hard lessons, but hopefully they'd pay off one day. Despite a major career change, and less fame, he was now so cautious of women and their intentions he could almost sign up to work in a monastery. Almost. He still enjoyed women, as long as they kept their mouths shut when it came to his past and wealth. So far they'd all had one feature in common: they thought he needed them more than he did.

Yet here he was, getting wound up over Brooke, whom he'd met only a few hours ago. A few hours that had included danger, saving someone, and the most exciting sex he'd had in forever. They were going at breakneck speed with getting to know each other. He should get up and head over to the other house, stay away from this distraction before she became more endearing. Before she got any deeper into his soul, because there would only be one ending, and he really did not want to face it with Brooke. Not that he could explain that to himself.

She fascinated him with her determination to get on with whatever had to be done, without stopping to make sure he was following. She'd been rattled in the house and again outside when the hill slid down towards them, but she'd dug in and continued doing what she'd set out to accomplish. And then she'd fallen into his arms and made out like he was the only man on the planet.

Long may it last, and he grinned.

Except he shouldn't be so idiotic. He sighed. High expectations always tipped over the edge into darkness.

CHAPTER FOUR

LYING IN FRONT of the fire where she'd just had fast, mind-blowing sex with a near stranger, Brooke stretched her legs as far as they'd go—not as far as she'd like—and raised her arms over her head. Incredible. To think she'd been wary of the guy when he'd first appeared. But Danny wasn't a stranger, not any more. If she could be so intimate with him, then he was in her blood now. Possibly only for a few hours, or even a couple of days, which was probably as far as this would go. They knew nothing about each other. Although that wasn't strictly true.

They were both medics, and were good at what they did, if helping Lloyd had shown her anything.

They had helped one another out of the mud and water whenever either of them got stuck or fell.

They both enjoyed a whisky. Of which neither of them had had more than a sip. She smiled to herself.

Their bodies had recognised each other in a flash of heat and desire—as if they'd been waiting for one another. She looked at the man who'd woken her up so thoroughly.

What they'd had added up to far more than the last man she'd dated and had a dull round of sex with. Her smile grew wide. Yeah, she'd just had an amazing experience. Now she'd better go remove the mud from her face and hair, then put on some clothes because the air was getting cooler as she lay naked on the floor. First the fire needed more wood.

Sitting up, she found Danny's gaze on her. 'I'm going to take a shower. Then I might heat up some soup.' Suddenly she felt awkward and wanted to cover up, but all that was on hand were her wet, muddy clothes she'd dumped in a pile as they'd got intense. It wasn't as though he made her feel inadequate or unattractive. It was... It was because she suddenly felt overwhelmed by the way they'd connected so fast and had seemed to be able to read each other without trying. If they were like that physically, how would it go on other levels? She would like to find a man to share her life with, one who'd accept her for herself, but it wasn't something that would come easily. She'd tried, and been disappointed, become cautious. Possibly too cautious. The disappointment was worse than not trying, so she'd given up and got on with doing the things she loved, like work, and more work, preferring that to being disenchanted again and again.

Danny's finger ran down her arm. 'You're getting goosebumps.'

'So are you.' The hairs on his arms were standing up too. Getting cold, or overheating with need?

Then he smiled, and her world tipped on its axis when he said, 'Go get warm and clean. I'll head over to where I'm staying and do the same. Am I invited to share the soup? I can bring bread rolls.'

Definitely a charmer. But that was okay as long as he didn't overdo it.

'See you shortly.' She pushed to her feet, fully aware of him watching as she straightened, making her feel wanted. He probably wanted more sex. She did, no hesitation. There wasn't going to be much going on for the rest of the day, apart from checking out the situation up on the road, so why not think they might get together again?

'You've got some bruises from those crash landings you took.' Danny touched her thigh and butt.

'I'm not surprised.'

Walking out of the room, her backside seemed to have a mind of its own, sort of wiggling in a sexy way. Her over-kissed lips presumed a smile. Sexy, or looking silly? Who cared? She wasn't a beauty queen, nor did she care. She'd leapt in and had sex with him, and that was huge. That was not something she'd normally do. Which went to show she trusted him to be good to her, physically at least. There might be time later on to learn more about him. She wasn't getting in a quandary about that at the moment.

By the time Brooke pushed the tap off in the shower her skin was wrinkled and red, but did she feel good. She'd applied a treatment to her hair after washing out a ton of mud. After rubbing moisturiser on her face, then doing the same for her arms and legs, she dried her hair into its neat bob, applied a light coating of make-up and went to get dressed, laughing at herself all the time. Make-up? Out here where the only person she'd probably see was Danny, and it was a little late to be trying to look her best. He'd seen her slip-sliding in the mud and water, crawling through a window into Lloyd's house. And naked by the fire.

Lloyd. How was he doing? Were they already operating on his ankle? What about the other injuries? Oh, no. Lloyd. Brad. She hadn't called Brad to let him know about his grandfather.

Picking up her phone, she tapped the number she'd found earlier in her father's notebook.

'Hello?'

Deep breath. 'Hi, Brad. It's Brooke.'

'Ahh, she deigns to ring me. It must be my lucky day.' Sarcasm was another one of his talents.

'Your grandfather has been taken to hospital.'

'Which is why I'm sitting in Christchurch Airport waiting for a flight.'

So the hospital had contacted him. 'That's good. He'll be pleased to see you.' Hopefully. It wasn't her place to be the judge of that family's problems, but Lloyd did need someone by his side at the moment and since Brad's parents now lived in Rarotonga he was the only person available.

'Why are you calling me now, and not earlier? I'd have thought I deserved that much of your time. I'm presuming you're at the bay.'

'I am. You don't understand. It's a disaster area around here. Just going over to Lloyd's house took forever as there's so much debris in the way. The landslide that came down behind his house is huge.' Another deep breath, because that was what she'd done a lot of in the last years of their relationship. 'Brad, I hate to tell you, but Lloyd's house has been badly damaged when the hillside came down. The house's not safe any more. I doubt it can be repaired. Probably have to be pulled down.'

'A complete rebuild is long overdue. I don't get why Granddad was so stubborn about hanging on to the place when it's so out-of-date and too small for the family and friends to visit. At least something good's come out of his accident. I can get a place that I like to spend time at.'

You selfish git. Lloyd hasn't wanted to change a thing because his memories of Jean are in every corner, on every shelf, in every room, and you don't give a toss.

It also wasn't her place to say what was on her mind, but she'd have loved to.

'Brad, tell Lloyd I'll be in to see him as soon as I leave the bay. We don't know what state the road's in yet, but I'll go when I can get out.'

'Did you help him out of the house?'

'Yes. Me and a doctor staying at Mike's.'

'How was he? The hospital said something about a broken ankle and a head wound. They're going to do some X-rays to see if there was an internal injury of some sort.' Brad finally sounded worried and sad.

'He didn't want to leave, was worried about Jean.'

'She's not there, so what's his problem?'

Lost love. To think she'd once believed they might have shared lifelong love.

'He took a hard knock to his head when the microwave came off the shelf.' Lloyd hadn't been his usual gutsy self, not by a long shot.

'That would've hurt. Got to go. My flight's been called.'

She tried one last time to make Brad understand his grandfather's plight. 'He was very distressed. Shock will be a big part of that, but I saw how worried he was about not being able to stay with his memories of Jean.'

'He'll get over that when he starts feeling better. See you.' The phone went dead.

'Not if I see you first, you jerk.' She dropped her phone on the bench in disgust. How had she ever loved him?

'Someone rattle your cage?' Danny stood in the doorway, looking good enough to eat dressed in black jeans hugging his hips and a grey jersey that did nothing to obliterate her memory of the chest underneath. A bag of buns swung from his fingers.

'Lloyd's grandson.'

'You're not mates, then?'

'He's my ex.'

'That explains a lot. Still want my company? You can throw things at me if you need to get him out of your system. I'm pretty good at dodging flying objects.' His smile was kind and understanding.

Damn it, but she laughed. And as she did, Brad's selfishness disappeared from her mind. Done and dusted.

'I wouldn't waste my time or energy.' Brad wasn't worth it. 'Come in and close the door before all the warm air disappears outside.'

'The wind's dropped further. It's almost hard to believe how strong it's been.' He left his shoes on the porch and a jacket on a peg by the door, as though he felt right at home already.

This was getting a little interesting. Where would they go with this? How far?

'The rain's letting up at last. I'll take the four-wheel bike out later to see what the damage is along the road. For as far as I can get, that is.'

'Mind if I hitch a ride? Might as well see what I'm in for when I come to leave.' He placed the buns on the bench, then crossed to lift the lid on the pot warming on the firebox, leaned closer to sniff. 'Pea and ham. Great. You make it?'

'Found it in the freezer. Mum will've left it

there a few weeks ago, knowing Saskia and I were coming to stay.' Their mother did spoil them when it came to home comforts.

'To think I nearly didn't come to the Sounds this weekend. I'd have missed out on all the fun.' Danny picked up the two glasses of whisky they'd been sidetracked from earlier.

She glanced at the microwave clock. Much earlier. It was now gone two. Time did fly when you were having fun rescuing a neighbour and getting to know a stranger intimately.

Handing her one of the glasses, Danny said, 'To us and one heck of a morning.' His mouth was wearing that delicious smile.

'It had its highs and lows, for sure.' She sipped the liquor and sat down on one of the two recliner chairs on either side of the fire. 'Know which I prefer.' Though the high wouldn't have happened if she hadn't been wound tight over getting Old Man Duggan to safety while hoping the house wouldn't collapse completely, trapping them all inside.

'Me too.' Danny lowered his sexy butt onto the opposite chair. 'Even if you can get out in the next couple of days, are you going to stay on for the week as you'd originally planned?'

'Haven't had time to think about it. There is a fair amount of cleaning up to do outside, which I can't leave for Mum and Dad next time they come down. Think I'll get some of Lloyd's clothes out of his place to drop into hospital for him too.'

'We'll do that one together. Though we probably shouldn't go inside again. That house is a menace.'

'True. But I keep hearing Lloyd calling for Jean and I want to give him something that's familiar to cling to. Maybe a photo of their wedding.'

'He's still got those? That says a lot about their relationship.'

'They were so close it was awesome to see.' So lovely, and she'd truly believed she'd have that with Brad. Silly woman. But there you go. Not everything turned out as expected in this world. She'd get it right next time—if she met the right man. Her eyes slid to the one sitting opposite, and a warmth bubbled through her. He mightn't be the one, but she could enjoy the time they did have together.

'Have you always been a paramedic?' he asked.

'I qualified as a medical laboratory tech, did that for six years. During that period I volunteered as an ambulance officer and found I loved it so much I swapped careers. I like helping people hands on, not from sitting behind a microscope.' She'd always been a caring kind of girl, looking out for pets, birds that flew into windows, or other kids at school when they hurt themselves at playtime. She should have known from the beginning that working in a lab wasn't her. 'I enjoy the intensity of the situations we go to. They keep me on my toes, and at my absolute best.' People died on her watch in the ambulance service, and it got to her, but somehow she coped because a lot more people made it home again, not only because of her but because of the way she helped their recovery. 'What did you do before setting out to become a doctor?'

He winced. 'I tried a few things, got into sport for a while, then decided it was time to settle down and get on with what I really wanted to do.' Danny stared at the mat where they'd had sex earlier. 'My father encouraged me, said that he didn't believe in going from school to university and diving straight into a full-on career. He thought I needed to get some life skills and experiences under my belt first.'

'And did you?' He wasn't very forthcoming about himself. Should she be getting worried? Though why not sit back and enjoy his company? She wasn't committing to anything with him.

'Yes.' He sipped his whisky. 'And now I'm getting some more.'

He was looking everywhere but at her, shifting that butt on the chair as if a change of subject was required. She could do that for now, though it felt familiar—Danny not talking about himself as if he had something to hide. Strange when they had barely started getting to know each other. Should she be wary? Or give it a rest and go with the subject change? See where it led? She didn't know, which was odd in itself. She usually ran a mile from people who kept things from her.

'Where will you be living in Nelson?'

The relief was huge. His eyes lightened, his mouth softened and he looked directly at her again. 'I've rented a fully furnished apartment around the waterfront. I'll be there for about six months. I've been working in Blenheim since January.'

The same health board covered both regions. 'Nelson will be a lot busier than Blenheim, though I guess if you did your initial training in Melbourne it'll still seem quiet.'

'Friday and Saturday nights are the same in any hospital. Bedlam with drunks and motor vehicle accidents, to name a few of the problems we face.'

'And the drug-enhanced people demanding to be seen by doctors when they aren't urgent.

I hate dealing with those and dread weekend night shifts.'

'You'd have to be insane not to.' Danny was settling deeper into the chair, his fingers not so tight around his glass.

She followed suit and relaxed. To heck with her concerns—for now at least. She'd go with the flow and enjoy Danny's company on this storm-battered day when there was little else to do.

'My grandmother was a nurse, and she can't believe some of the stories I've told her about over-toasted patients and having to have security guards in the department.' The whisky was smooth on her tongue. The atmosphere was calming and quiet. Just right. Outside the tempest was dying, leaving behind the shambles it had created, going on to deliver more havoc elsewhere, hopefully out to sea.

Danny's laugh was deep and heart-warming. 'What I saw today when you were with Lloyd, I cannot picture you in a lab coat studying a blood film down a microscope.' He grinned. 'Nor does it compare with another picture I have of you.'

Heck. She blushed, bright red by the feel of the temperature charging up her neck to her cheeks. 'You are a right charmer, aren't you?' she said a little too sharply.

'You don't trust that?'

Breathe deep. 'Not always. Well and truly bitten, now totally averse.' Crikey, she was being honest, and saying things as they were when she didn't normally talk about private matters at all. Clearing the air before she got too interested in him?

'The grandson, for one?'

She should have kept her mouth shut. But then again, Brad was her history and she wasn't ashamed of her role in their relationship. 'Afraid so.' She got up to stir the soup. Dipped her finger in and didn't get burned. 'Not quite ready.' Crossing to the kitchen nook, she put the oven on to heat the buns, got out soup bowls and plates, cutlery and salt and pepper.

'Whereabouts in Nelson do you live?'

'I'm central and can walk into town for my coffee. I bought a little cottage on the bank of the Maitai River. It's a nineteen-twenties house, cold as a snow field in winter and warmer than this oven in summer, but I love it. The maintenance is ongoing.' She placed the cutlery and serviettes on the table.

'Want me to do anything?'

'I've got it, thanks.' Suddenly she felt awkward again. Who was this man? Like really, who was he? She'd had sex with him, was sharing a drink and soup, and didn't have the foggiest. For all she knew he could be lying about being a trainee doctor and using his charm to get whatever he wanted. There again, he knew Paula and Mike, a surgeon at Blenheim Hospital, and they wouldn't have left him in their bach if they didn't think he was trustworthy.

The soup spoons hit the table with a clang. She turned to look at Danny without blinkers on. He still looked good. Kind and caring. And charming, which wasn't a fault if used appropriately. He'd been gentle with her, then strong and sexy, and then gentle again.

'Brooke?' Danny stood in front of her, not in her space, giving her room. 'It's hitting home what we've done, isn't it?'

Was that it? Leaping to have sex with a stranger was new for her, yet at the time she'd known what she was doing and had still wanted it. After what they'd been through outside she'd needed that affirmation she was okay. But was she now looking for reasons to doubt herself? Or Danny?

'It's okay. I'll head back to the house and let you have some time to yourself.' No charm, no heart-melting smile, just a genuine look of understanding.

She watched him walk out of the door, her hands pressed to the tabletop. She shouldn't have had sex with him. Tell that to someone who believed her when she had felt so good afterwards. They'd both been coming down off an adrenaline high and it had felt right. Not that there'd been a lot of considering about what they'd been about to do. She'd just known she had to have him, and he'd appeared to have felt the same about her, which was a turn-on too, if she'd needed another one. He was so sexy. He'd been a generous lover. It hadn't been all about what he wanted. Was she being selfish, letting him walk out of the door because she was in a quandary about herself, and him?

Pulling out a chair, she sank onto it and put her elbows on the table to drop her chin into her hands. What a screwed-up woman she'd turned out to be. She'd just had the most amazing sex with a lovely man, make that a sexy, good-looking man, and now she was doubting herself.

Get over yourself, Brooke. Don't you want to find a man who'll treat you well and accept who you are? The only way that will happen is if you let go of the past and have some fun.

Was it that simple? Anyway, hadn't Danny come out to help her when he could've stayed in the house pretending nothing was going on? Didn't he just show how much he understood her by saying their moment on the mat was hitting home?

So what if he was charming? It could be a good thing, and it never hurt to be complimented once in a while. Didn't mean it came with a price tag. She had become a little twisted when it came to men. Time to change that.

Getting a grocery bag from a drawer, Brooke started packing it with everything she needed for lunch.

That went well, Danny thought as he stared into the fridge, trying to decide what he'd have for lunch now that soup was off the menu. Not a lot of choice in front of him. He'd come prepared with basics, but what had seemed good when he was in the supermarket now made him shake his head in disappointment. He could still smell pea and ham soup.

Closing the fridge, he plugged in the kettle for coffee and pulled out a stool to park his backside. No new messages on his phone since the one from his mate who owned this place asking how he'd fared overnight and if the property was still intact.

The house hadn't taken a hit. The yard had its share of debris, including small branches and lots of leaves, but otherwise it looked much as it had yesterday.

But he wasn't quite the same man who'd woken up this morning after a night of intermittent sleep while the house was being slammed with wind and rain. No, that guy had had a wake-up call in the form of one dark blonde woman with a slim, short frame, and a lot of determination. Determination and uncertainties. Strength and fears. He hadn't met her in anything close to normal circumstances, but she didn't seem overly fazed about getting to know more about him in a hurry, and when he'd backed off talking about himself she'd been quick to pick up on that and let him be. That alone earned her more points than just about anything a woman could do for him. The fantastic sex had been a bonus. If only she hadn't got cold feet. When they'd had sex they'd been coming down off a high of nerves and adrenaline, and it was only natural to reach out to each other.

More than reached out, as far as he was concerned. He'd mentioned the fact he'd been interested in sport before he took to studying medicine. He *never* said that to anyone who didn't already know. He was always on his guard. Not around Brooke, it seemed. Saying things like that always brought on more questions, or shocked surprise when the realisation dawned. 'You're *the* Daniel Collins, as in famous golfer.'

As in the egotist who went off the rails when his career disappeared overnight. Young and unable to cope with suddenly being incapable of hitting a golf ball with the accuracy that had won him many tournaments, he'd found fault with Iris and dropped her. Then he'd taken to dating every woman who glanced his way. He had used women to feed his ego, something he was now appalled about. Until his father had stepped in and made him look at himself with a frank and hard conversation about how he was letting everyone down, especially himself. Dad had followed up with a reminder of how he'd once dreamed of being a doctor and how that option was still there if he settled down and pulled his head in. That conversation had flipped his life around, possibly because deep down he'd wanted to be normal again.

Brooke hadn't a clue, and he liked that so much. Not that she knew him by any other name than Danny. If he did get to spend more time with her he'd have to fill her in about his past, but surely he was allowed to have some fun without turning it all on its head straight away? They had only met that morning, and once he left here they probably wouldn't see each other again except at work.

Yeah, right, who was he fooling? He wanted to see a lot more of her. Was it possible that once she knew about him, Brooke still wouldn't care two hoots about the money he'd earned and how he was still put on a pedestal all these years later? She appeared to hold herself tall without needing to lean on someone else's accolades to get through life. She didn't shy away from problems or blink coquettishly at him. Then again, he'd seen it all before. Yeah, he sighed, he was jaded.

But he sensed there might be more to Brooke that he'd enjoy being a part of, sharing good times and the bad stuff that life might toss at them. There was a depth to her he hadn't encountered in a long while. Obviously she'd also taken some knocks. The grandson was not on her Christmas list by the fed-up look in her eyes as she'd hung up from talking to him. Nothing like her feelings for the grandfather. There'd been nothing but care and concern as Brooke saw to that man's needs.

She could care for his too—as much as she liked. Except he didn't really have any other than wanting a life partner somewhere along the way to old age. A woman to share everything with, and possibly have a family together.

Here he went—getting ahead of himself. She'd been happy for him to walk away from lunch, hadn't tried to call him back. She'd got the jitters. It was plain in her face and how her hands kept flexing against her thighs. Funny, because it so rarely happened, but he'd known when he wasn't wanted. Another point to mark up in her favour. She wasn't all about doing whatever it took to make him happy.

Which made him very happy indeed.

Knock-knock.

Hope soared. It had to be Brooke. Who else would be out and about in this weather? There was only one way to find out. Before she disappeared on him because obviously he wasn't interested in opening the door to her.

'Brooke.' His heart did a little skip. 'Here, let me take that.' He reached for the pot she was holding in one hand. From the fingers of the other swung a laden bag. 'How did you manage to knock on the door?'

Her pert nose screwed up as she laughed. 'Used my heel.'

'Come in.'

'There's too much soup for me.' An olive branch by any other name.

'I'm glad. I wasn't getting enthused over what's in the fridge.' He closed the door behind her and followed her into the kitchen with a bounce in his step. Sometimes things had a way of working out. He was going to hang on to that idea for as long as possible. He might even thank the weather gods for sending the storm, if not for the people who'd been injured or lost property or would be stranded for days to come.

'Didn't you bring food with you?' Brooke was looking at him in surprise. 'You're not exactly within walking distance of a supermarket out here, even on a good day.'

'There's plenty here, just nothing I fancied after the idea of hot soup grabbed me.'

'That's better. For a moment I thought you were saying you didn't prepare for your stay, though I can't imagine Paula not making certain you were left with everything you'd need.'

So Brooke thought he might be a bit useless when it came to looking after himself, did she?

'I am very self-reliant. I've had to be.' Whenever he couldn't face being accosted by ardent fans at the supermarket or a takeaway outlet, usually after another tedious news slot on television or in the internet media.

Unpacking the bag she'd brought with her, she handed him the half-full glass of whisky he'd put aside when he left her house. 'Here, can't have you saying I neglected you.'

Obviously not a wasteful woman then. Because she had to be careful? Or didn't believe in acting like a spoilt child? Whichever, he liked that about her. Removing the plastic wrap she'd sealed the glass with, he laughed. 'I've never taken so long to finish one drink. Did you bring yours?'

Reaching into the bag, she lifted out another half-full glass. 'I don't usually overindulge, but today is like no other I've encountered. Not for a long time, anyhow. Cheers.' Her lips were soft on the rim of her glass.

'Cheers.' He joined her in savouring the whisky. 'I'll put that pot on to heat a bit more.' He wasn't in any hurry to eat. She might leave the moment her bowl was empty, and he didn't want that. It had been a long time since he'd enjoyed a woman's company so much, so why cut it short if he didn't have to?

Brooke sat at the table, crossed her legs and focused on him. Not in a *What's in this for me?* way, but with an open and honest look, as though she genuinely wanted to get to know what made him tick. 'You said you've had to be self-reliant. In what way?'

There wasn't much Brooke seemed to miss. He'd be wise to remember that. 'Just a few hiccups along the way. Life throwing its curve balls at me, as it does everyone,' he added in an attempt to divert her away from him in particular.

'Know what you mean.'

He'd got away with it. The sudden tension backed off. 'Like today for Lloyd.'

'I hope he survives this. Not the injuries he sustained, but the loss of his home and those wonderful memories of Jean.' She sipped her drink. 'My largest curve ball was Brad, the grandson. But he's firmly in the past now.'

Hadn't the man wound her up tight during that phone call earlier?

'You see him occasionally down here?'

'Not if I can help it. I do my best to avoid him just to save hearing all the reasons why I'm such a cow. I take it you're single or we wouldn't have got close earlier. Or am I being naïve?' Her eyes had become very focused on him.

Where did that come from? Had Brad cheated on her? 'I'm definitely single, and no, I would not have touched you, let alone made love, if I'd been in a relationship.'

'Thank you.' She sipped her drink. 'You didn't come to New Zealand to get away from someone, did you?'

And he thought he'd distracted her. A whole load of someones was the answer he wasn't sharing.

'No.'

Then she blushed, and sputtered, 'I'm sorry. Take no notice of me. I'm being nosey. It's just that I don't usually let any man near so quickly and I'm trying to figure out why I did with you.' Her elbow banged on the top of the table. 'Now I'm talking too much.'

Had he got to her in a similar way to how she'd got to him? It would be kind of fun if he had. If he wasn't looking for something that wasn't there just because this didn't usually happen to him.

'Perhaps I'd better dish up the soup after all.'

'You think a mouthful of pea and ham will shut me up?' Her mouth curved into a soft grin.

A grin that went straight to his gut and sent tendrils of longing spiralling through him.

'I can always hope so.' He remained on his chair and sipped his whisky. 'How often have you been caught out here by a storm?'

'Only once before and it wasn't as severe as this one. The roading gangs had the slips cleared within twenty-four hours. I have a feeling we're going to be stuck for longer than that. You might have to call in the water taxi when it comes time to leave if it's really bad around here. That'll get you to Havelock, but what you do about getting to Nelson I don't know. There's probably a bus going through from Blenheim.'

'I'll worry about that when I know what we're dealing with.' He'd need his car in Nelson, if at all possible. 'This is a new experience for me.'

'How long have you been working in New Zealand?'

'Six months. My initial term with the local health board is for a year, but I'm thinking of asking for an extension. This is a great region, with the Sounds and the vineyards. I like the smaller towns too.'

'Careful. You'll be settling down permanently before you know it.'

Not likely. The whole idea of stopping in one place permanently was ideal, if not on his agenda. People would invariably find out who he was and then he'd lose the comfort of being anonymous. Glancing at Brooke, he had to admit it mightn't be so bad with a woman at his side he could trust to accept him for who he was and not only for what had made him famous.

'I'm not ready for that.' Yet here he was, only hours after meeting Brooke and having the strangest thoughts about what might lie ahead. For the first time he wasn't ducking for cover, instead felt they were level pegging so far.

'Did you grow up in Melbourne?'

'Victoria.' He instantly regretted his terse answer. Another ingrained habit.

'Plenty of vineyards there too.' That eagle look was on him again. She knew he was avoiding giving her a specific answer. But to say Ballarat might start some bells ringing inside that lovely head that he wasn't ready to deal with.

'Some superb reds are made there.'

'So you'll return to Australia to further your studies?'

'Probably. Once I finish my medical degree I intend qualifying as a radiologist.'

Her eyes widened. 'Radiology? I thought that was for medics who didn't want to have too much interaction with patients.'

'Yes, and you have doubts about that?' X-rays couldn't ask him questions about golf or saving Toby Frank. They'd show him what was wrong with a patient, and he'd pass that on to the doctor dealing with the patient.

A frown had formed on Brooke's brow. 'Here I was thinking how personable you are. But then I have been known to get my people reading skills wrong.'

'Haven't we all?' Danny tried for a laugh

to lighten the heaviness settling in his gut. It didn't come off. Brooke was right. He did have the gift of the gab—because he liked people, was interested in what made them tick, and had a way of drawing them out. Of course that was when they weren't trying to dig into his background. Draining his glass, he rose to get their lunch. He'd dodged enough bullets for now.

CHAPTER FIVE

'Your mum makes a great soup,' Danny said as he scraped up the last smear from the bowl with a piece of bun. 'Delicious.'

'I agree.' Brooke leaned back in her chair, feeling the most relaxed since she'd gone to bed last night to the sound of the wind ripping through trees and hitting the house.

'Tea, coffee, whisky or wine?'

'Tea, thanks. I'll wait until after we've done a recce of the road for something stronger. Though it might be a short ride if there's a slip beyond the bay on the way back to the main road.' The only good thing about the slip that had come down while they were outside was that it hadn't blocked the road in that direction. No doubt there'd be a lot of people living further out who wouldn't agree with her.

'What are the chances there haven't been any other landslides?'

'Zilch. Big storms nearly always cause slips

around here, and this one was exceptionally rough.'

'All part of living in such a beautiful place, I suppose. Sitting here, looking out over the bay towards the Sound beyond, it's hard to imagine scenery more stunning.'

'It's a great location.' A perfect bolthole too. She and Saskia came here whenever they needed a break from work or other problems. It was here, walking on the beach for hours, that she'd chosen moving on from Brad to regain control over her life. For her, moving on with life had meant stopping still, having one job to get totally involved in without waiting for the axe to fall, and settling into her small cottage and making changes to it that were for her and not the next person to live there. To be able to plant daffodil bulbs and be there to see them flower in the next spring. To choose colours that she liked for her curtains, not what would appeal to a prospective buyer when she'd finished redecorating the house.

'Did your family spend all your summers here when you were growing up?' Danny brought her back to now.

'We did. Dad would go back to work after two weeks, but he always returned for the weekends. It was much the same with most of the bachs in the area. I've still got friends from those days. Of course everyone's now scattered across the country, even around the world, so we don't catch up often, but when we do it's usually one heck of a party.'

Strange how Danny wanted to know about her time here but when she'd asked where he came from his reply had been Victoria, one of Aussie's states. He hadn't mentioned where he lived in that vast area. It *was* as if he didn't want to talk about himself, which bugged her. She wanted to know more about him, even understood she might be rushing him if she dived in with questions, but it still irked. If they were spending time together, what was wrong with talking about himself a little? He reminded her how often people close to her had kept things from her.

She would never forget that day her mother had picked her up from school and said, 'You love those stories about girls in boarding schools, don't you?'

If only she'd known what was coming, she'd have answered differently, said, *No, Mum, I hate them*. Instead she'd said, 'Yes,' and had got home to find her bag packed and two air-line tickets to Auckland on her dressing table. One for her mother, and one for her. At least Mum had gone with her to the school, explaining it was an opportunity for Brooke to get away from those bullies.

But what if Danny was hiding something important from her? Or was she looking for trouble because of her past? Not everyone kept important things from her, but she was braced to look for it.

Dishes clattered into the sink. Brooke jerked around to see Danny rinsing their bowls. 'Sorry, I was miles away.' She needed to take a break from worrying about who he was and what was behind his abrupt answers to some of her questions—for now anyway.

'Teach me for asking about your family summers.' He wore a gentle smile but there was contrition in his eyes, as though he regretted it even when he couldn't know what he might have triggered. Could be that he understood being hurt by someone you loved.

She wasn't asking who. That was getting too personal too soon, she supposed. Not that she'd held back over Brad, but that was her way of dealing with her past.

'Shall I get the bike?' Why was she asking? She was supposed to be doing as she saw fit, not getting permission. Those days were over. 'What I mean is, are you ready to go for a look-see?'

'You bet.' His eyes lit up in anticipation.

'It might be the shortest trip you've had any-where,' she warned despite the happiness spilling through her, brought on by this man, who seemed to tweak her strings in good *and* worrying ways.

'You're a dab hand at driving a four-wheel bike? I'm not risking life or limb?' He was grinning at her as if she was the best thing to happen along today.

'Never driven one before.' Her dad had taught her to ride a smaller, less powerful bike when she was nine. Far too young, her mother had said, which had made her more determined to do it and she had become very proficient very quickly, impressing her father and winning a few extra hugs.

'Then I'm in for an adventure,' Danny said with a laugh, obviously not believing her.

'If I were you, I'd delve through the gum-boots at the back door for some that might fit. We'll probably end up tracking through more mud at some point.' She'd take a shovel in case they lost footwear, but with their height gum-boots were easier to retrieve.

'I'll join you shortly. Unless you need a hand getting the bike out?'

'No, I'm good. There doesn't appear to be anything preventing access there.' She still had to get that gas bottle before the day was out.

Danny could give her a hand. More getting stuck and muddy and needing a hot shower. More getting close and—

Stop it. Go get the bike.

For all she knew, Danny mightn't want a repeat of earlier. She shouldn't either. She should be getting to know him better before thinking of stripping naked again. Her skin tingled at the thought of his fingers teasing her and his lips kissing trails all over her breasts. Mentally flapping her hand in front of her overheating face, she headed for the cool air outside. There was a time and place for everything, and this wasn't it for having repeat sex with Danny. Which was a huge shame. She grinned and hummed a tune as she collected her coat and gumboots, and the keys for the shed and bike. Danny would have to sit behind her, his thighs on either side of hers, hopefully his arms around her waist—though that wasn't necessary it would feel good.

The bike bumped over the lawn as Brooke drove towards the road, avoiding branches and other debris. 'The road's full of ruts,' she said over her shoulder to Danny—who *was* tucked in close to her back, and yes, he did have one arm around her waist. Oh, so cosy. She grinned like the proverbial cat with the cream.

'There's been a lot of water running across

to the beach,' he said right beside her ear, his breath teasing her skin.

'Still is compared to normal. Hold on.' Revving the motor, Brooke negotiated a deep gouge and a small rise taking them onto the road. Turning left, she started along the road.

Nearly a kilometre on, just around a tight corner, they came to an abrupt halt. The hillside had come across the road and down into the sea fifty metres below. Massive trees were contained in the clay and rock, and over the road and down the bank to the tempestuous water.

'There's our answer,' Danny said as he swung a leg over the back of the bike and stood up in ankle-deep mud. 'We're not going any further today.'

Switching off the bike, Brooke surveyed the sight before her. He was right. Nothing or no one was getting over that slip in a hurry. 'It's going to take heavy equipment to shift that,' she agreed. 'I'm going to try and see what's on the other side.' She started for the slip and a large pine tree stuck on the side.

'Brooke, that's not a good idea. What if there's more hillside to come down? Or a boulder or two?'

She stared up the hill. 'I don't think that'll

happen. It's clear above this. You can see the rock face now.'

'Yeah, and I don't want to be pulling your broken body off there if you're wrong. Don't do it.' Seemed he could be bossy when he chose.

But he might have a point. She didn't do standing back and waiting for help to arrive very easily though. Her motto was to get in and do it herself, and all she wanted to know was how bad this blockage was.

'I'll only be walking across.'

Danny's hand took hers in a gentle grip. 'Yes, and I'll only be holding my breath and wondering what would happen if you slipped and went over the edge into the sea.'

His look was serious and made her draw a breath.

'Fair enough. Anyway, even if I got across there's no knowing where the next slip is. I can't hear diggers at work so I'm picking they're working near the start of the road.'

'Is there anyone you can ring to find out what's happening?' He was still holding her hand.

She kept still, enjoying the warm, firm grip and the hot tingles on her skin. 'There's a local company that does work with diggers and bull-dozers that is usually called in to help when-ever something like this happens. But I don't know the family personally so I'm not going to harass them when they're probably getting lots of calls while trying to get on with whatever needs doing.'

'Fair enough.' Danny didn't appear at all worried that he might be stuck here for a few days.

'When did you say you start at Nelson ED?'

'Monday afternoon.' A flicker of concern crossed his face. 'I'll give them a call tomorrow to let them know my situation, and I'll also find out about water taxis and buses then. It looks too rough for any boat to come into your bay today, but hopefully it'll have calmed down some by later tomorrow or Monday morning.'

'What about Mike? He might be able to sort out transport to Nelson for you.'

'I'll add him to the list of calls.'

She leaned her head to one side. 'You're obviously comfortable with how things are today.' It wasn't bothering her as she had all week for the road to be cleared enough to get out, and neither did she mind being here alone.

'Couldn't be better,' he said with a grin. 'I'm happy to be out of—' He stopped, drew a breath. 'Happy having some time without patients and emergencies to distract me.'

Once again he'd cut himself off from saying

what he'd first intended. Interesting. There was more to this man than she was getting. But for now she wasn't pushing, which was so unlike her these days. It seemed she wanted to enjoy his company more than to be wary of him.

'Now that Lloyd's safely tucked up in a hospital bed, you mean?' She couldn't stop grinning right back at him. What was it about Danny that had her reacting in ways she thought she'd forgotten? She should be acting more cautiously, not ready to dive right in and make the most of him.

He started walking towards the edge of the road where it dropped away to the beach that was being pounded by an angry sea, his hand still wrapped around hers. 'There seems to be a lot of logs and trees heading this way.'

'They'll be from the Pelorus River. Most of the tree trunks on our beach come from there after even a small storm or high tides. Some locals cut them up for firewood.'

'Doesn't the salt cause rust in their fireboxes?'

'That's why my dad isn't a fan of driftwood for our fire. He's had to replace ours twice after the chimney split due to heavy rust.'

'Look at that sea. It's relentless.'

'The power of nature is amazing and frightening at times.' She admired the natural forces she saw here. The wind, tide and rain made changes large and small all the time. 'Let's hope we get a clear sky tonight and you can see the sky like you've never seen it before. Unless you live out in the back of beyond back home, that is.' She paused, got no answer, so continued, thinking he was definitely keeping quiet about his private life. Why? It was starting to grate. Was she being impatient? On a disgruntled sigh, she let it go. 'There are so many stars above us it's incredible. I love nothing more than to lie on the beach and just stare upwards.'

'I haven't had the opportunity to see that. But the chance of a clear sky tonight is nigh on impossible, surely?'

'You'll be surprised how quickly the clouds will clear away, unless there's more bad weather to come, and when I checked earlier it seems we're done for now.' No one needed any more rain, not for weeks at least. There was water everywhere. Water. Of course. It was the first thing she should have thought of. 'I need to check the house tank and the supply pipe from up the hill.'

'Aren't you on a community system?'

He had to be a city man to ask that. 'No one out here is. We all collect our water from uphill streams or underground sources. Ours comes from underground, but the pipe is above ground and could've been damaged by falling trees.' It was always her father's first priority to check the water flow to their tanks after a storm or earthquake. She'd been distracted more than she'd realised. Her elbows hugged her sides as her body smiled. Who'd have thought that amidst the carnage and noise and mayhem of the past twenty-odd hours she'd have been distracted by a sexy man? Also a kind, understanding, gentle man. That said a lot about him. Or her life. Her feet were light on the ground as she headed to the bike. 'Let's head back.'

Danny climbed back on the bike, his arm again around her waist.

'No quick fix for this,' she said.

'I hadn't quite grasped the extent of the damage.' His sigh tickled her neck. 'I might be a day or two late getting back to my real life.'

'If the sea drops further I can launch Dad's boat and take you to Havelock rather than getting the taxi.'

'How will you get the boat out of the water on your own when you return?'

'There's a winch on the tractor.' But the water would have to be calm or she'd be struggling to align the boat with the rollers on the trailer.

'I'll call the taxi if necessary.' He spoke in a don't-argue-with-me way.

Brooke grinned. 'Yes, boss.' Pressing the starter, she headed back to the house.

'Glad you understand,' he said close to her ear, his breath sending tendrils of heat over her neck.

'Um…would you mind checking the water system with me?' *Or shall we head inside and get warm together again?* 'If I find a break in one of the joins my hands aren't strong enough to put it back together. Especially when water is rushing through it.'

'Of course I'm coming with you.'

She softened some more towards Danny, let go some of the angst about how he dodged answering her questions in depth. He was so easy to get along with and didn't make a big deal about helping her. *Early days, Brooke, early days.* Besides, who said this encounter with Danny was going anywhere? A great bit of sex, some time together checking out the results of the storm, sharing soup and a drink, didn't add up to something deep and meaningful, or even the beginning of such. More likely, come tomorrow or Monday and they'd be saying, 'Bye, see you around.'

In the meantime, he was going to give her a hand.

'Thanks. First, I'll see if the water is coming through. We might not have to do anything else.'

Not so much as a trickle dripped from the outside tap. The pipe leading down from the water source sounded hollow when Brooke tapped it further along.

'Dad keeps a small backpack ready with wrenches and screwdrivers and replacement fittings. I'll go grab it.'

'Gumboots all right for this?' Danny asked.

'Maybe not. We're going over rocks and through a waterway that's higher than normal. Gummies won't have enough grip.'

Footwear changed, the pack on Danny's back, they set off, following the pipe up the hill. When it went under the road, Brooke led him across the other side where it was again visible. Every fifty metres or so, she tapped the pipe to see if it was still empty. As the climb got steeper, their feet slipped and slid on the wet ground, making the going slower.

'There.' Danny pointed to the other side of the racing stream. 'Is that what you're looking for?'

'Where?' Brooke followed the direction he was pointing at. One end of a black pipe was bobbing on the edge of the water. 'Got it. That's what we're after. Now to find the other

end and see if we've still got the connection.'
Thankful her father was always prepared and
that there were five connectors in the pack, she
began to step through the water, watching for
unsteady rocks to avoid.

'There's the other end,' Danny called behind
her. 'It's caught in a tree.'

Reaching the first piece, which was coming
from further up the hill, Brooke lifted it and
grunted with relief. 'This appears to be the
only fault. Water's flowing fast. But it means
reconnecting the joiner will be difficult.' She
was glad Danny was with her.

'There's only half a connector on this end.'
He dragged the pipe free and walked it up to
her.

'There's a spare in the pack.' She reached
for it, touching his shoulder with her fingers
as she caught the strap. Not that he'd have felt
it with the heavy wet weather jacket he wore.

Danny turned and locked his eyes on her.
'You think?'

So he might have sensed her hand on his
shoulder. Yes, she'd like some more time with
him, but that didn't come in a pack. Time to be
serious and stop wondering what could happen
if she let her guard down some more. Not that
it was anywhere near as high as usual.

'I know.'

'Damn.' His grin was infectious.

It went a way to lowering that guard further, and she grinned back. How great it would be to have a man to spend time with outside of work, to share meals and a bed, to talk about anything and everything with, and even argue sometimes. So far, she was enjoying Danny. But first impressions weren't always totally true. Brad had been a charmer and full of fun when they'd been getting together. No change from the boy she'd known on the family summer trips here when she was growing up. There'd been no inkling how he'd turn out. Same as her first boyfriend, all fun and excitement until he got what he wanted.

'Here.' She handed Danny the connector. 'Have you ever used one of these before?'

'Can't say I have.' He took it and pulled the two sections apart. Definitely not a country boy or he wouldn't have done that so abruptly.

'Careful. Don't lose the O-rings.'

'Sorry. Tell me what to do.'

Within minutes they had the pipe fixed and the lower section weighing heavily in Brooke's hand. 'I'll wait a few minutes to make sure the supply doesn't run out because of another break further up.' Hopefully there wasn't. She was ready to head home to the warmth. It was getting colder here under the trees showering them with water with every gust of wind. The afternoon was closing in and soon night would fall, lowering the temperature further.

'You know what you're doing, don't you?' Danny looked at her with something like admiration.

'Comes with growing up here. Dad made Saskia and me learn about this and many other things that kept the house running because we never knew when it could go wrong and being so far from town isn't always ideal.' She'd put extra effort into making sure she was *au fait* with the essentials in an attempt not to be sent away to boarding school every year, but her mother always won out on that one. 'Right, let's go home and get warm and dry.'

It wasn't so easy going down, with water and mud making traction harder than it had been on the way up, but finally they walked out of the bush at the edge of the road.

'That wasn't what I expected to be doing during my stay in the Sounds.' Danny laughed as he crossed the road and stepped off into mud. He sank up to his ankle, then his calf, and higher. 'Great.' He wrenched his leg hard and groaned as a loud popping sound reached Brooke.

'What's happened?' she asked.

His mouth was tight, his hands clenched on his thighs.

'Danny?' She reached him, keeping clear of where his leg was buried.

'I've wrenched my knee. It's a bit painful,' he gasped.

So he wouldn't be pulling his leg free, not easily anyway. 'Keep still and I'll try to scoop the mud away.'

'Get a trowel or spade.' His voice was strained.

'No, I'm doing it as fast as possible.' He was in pain and the sooner she freed him the better.

'You'll wreck your fingers doing it by hand.'

'Too bad.' Mud flew as she scraped around his trouser-covered leg.

Above her, Danny was alternately holding his breath and groaning.

'I'm getting there.'

Scoop, splat. Scoop, splat.

A fingernail tore. 'Is the pain only in your knee?'

'Yes.'

'One to ten? Which is it?'

'Five.'

Bad but bearable. If he was being honest. 'Right, there's your shoe. I'm going to try and free it without putting any pressure on your leg.'

'I'll try lifting it.'

'No, Danny. That'll only add to the pain level. We'll do it my way.' She already had most of the shoe exposed and began digging underneath with her fingers. Another nail broke. Time for a manicure when she got out of the bay. 'Right, here we go. No, wait. I'll remove more mud from in front of your foot so you don't have to bend your knee.'

He huffed out a breath. 'Glad you're thinking clearly. I don't think I can bend it at the moment. Wonder if I've dislocated the kneecap again.'

'You've done this before?' Using a flat rock, she scraped a narrow trough from the foot to the top of the ground.

'Unfortunately, yes, a few years back. But it's usually a quick fix, and I'll soon be fully mobile.'

'Though in some pain.' She'd seen patients with dislocated knees and kneecaps. The kneecap was a better option, easier to get moving after it was put back in place, but painful discomfort came with that.

'I have painkillers.'

'I know, remember?'

'Of course. Lloyd.'

'What are they for?'

'In case something like this happens.'

That was all she was going to find out. He

certainly didn't talk about himself. Did that mean the pills were his, not in case someone else needed them? If she got into questions he might head back to the other house without her. Once he could walk, that was.

'After we've got your foot free I'll get the bike to take you down to the house.'

He shook his head. 'I'll take a look at it before you do that. It might be as easy as straightening my leg to fix it and then I'll be able to hobble across the lawn.'

'I've seen that done a couple of times.' She'd also seen the pain that happened as the cap moved back into place. 'I agree the sooner we do that the better off you'll be.' She sat back on her haunches, ignoring the cold where her trousers were now wet through. 'Let's get you unstuck. I'll lift your leg. You try to remain loose and relaxed.'

He touched her shoulder, gave her a gentle squeeze. 'I'm ready. Get on with it.'

Placing her hands palm up under his lower leg, she counted, 'One, two, three.' Pushing firmly without jerking, she raised his leg, bringing his foot free.

'That was nice,' Danny grunted. 'Right, can I put an arm around you for balance while I straighten my leg?'

'Don't you want to take a look to make sure it is dislocated first?'

'I'd have to drop my jeans and that wouldn't be easy standing on one leg.'

'Fair enough.' He seemed to know what he was doing. Brooke moved beside him, wound an arm around his waist.

His fingers were tense as they wrapped over her shoulder. 'Here we go.' Without any hesitation Danny straightened his leg. The knee gave a loud popping sound. Danny groaned louder, his fingers digging into her shoulder.

The knee popping suggested he'd fixed the problem, but she'd still check his knee once they were inside. 'You need to elevate your leg and put ice around it.'

'True,' he muttered through a stalled breath.

'Let's go to my place. It's closer. There's ice and chicken casserole in the freezer, and I'll make you a drink to warm you up.'

'I'm all for that. Could you get my toilet bag for me? I put the painkillers back in it.'

'No problem.'

He took a step, paused. 'Actually, no, I'll get it.'

'You're going to walk an extra hundred metres when I can get your bag?' What was he so reticent about her seeing? 'Worried I might go through your bag?' Tempting as it was, she wouldn't.

'Of course not,' he said hurriedly.

Too quick? Her stomach clenched. She wanted to believe he wasn't hiding anything, but history taught her differently.

'Would you prefer to go to the other house?' she asked sharply.

'I'm being an idiot. Sorry.' He looked repentant, as if he finally understood he'd upset her.

'It really doesn't matter which house we go to. I'm not leaving you on your own.'

Danny grimaced. He'd walked into that one. Too eager to hide his identity, he'd suddenly worried Brooke might open his toilet bag to get the pill bottle and read his name on the label—Daniel Collins. She might recognise it. Or she mightn't, but she could look him up on the internet.

Or it was possible she'd do neither, and carry on treating him as she'd been doing so far. Why was it so hard to accept Brooke might be unfazed by who he might be and liked who she'd met? He wasn't used to it. That was why. There were times when he met a woman and the reaction was similar to Brooke's, until they learned more about him. Right now the last thing he wanted was Brooke changing towards him. This could only last until they were away from here, maybe for a while longer, but it would come to an end and, more than anything, he'd like to have made some inroads with her, so she knew he was more than that public image.

'Hello, Danny? You listening?'

To trust or not to trust? The million-dollar question. Breathe in, hold, breathe out. He looked at Brooke, drank in the genuine concern for him in her eyes and sighed. Sometimes he just had to take a chance.

'I'd love to doss down at your place, and yes, if you'd get my bag that'd be great.'

'That wasn't so hard, was it?' she said with a smile.

His heart lightened. *If only you knew.* But for once he was glad he was risking everything. Brooke could prove to be worth it.

'Want to hobble down to your house with me?'

Those golden-green eyes lightened and her smile grew as she took a firmer hold around his waist. 'Best invitation I've had all day.'

'Doesn't say much for your day then,' he said through the pain radiating out from his knee. It would soon improve enough to be able to move more freely. Last time he'd been about to tee off for a friendly match between club mates when someone shouted a warning about a snake coming onto the ground. He'd spun around without moving his right leg and pop went the kneecap. It hadn't taken long to recover fully, and this would be the same. The pain was annoying more than anything.

'Anything else I can grab while I'm at it? Those clothes look a sight.'

His wet jeans clung to him, making him shiver. On the plus side, that might help with any swelling. 'My overnight bag's in the bedroom with everything I need, except my phone, which should be on the table.'

He hobbled up the step to Brooke's back door where, to his embarrassment, she insisted he sit while she knelt to remove his shoes. He held his breath and pretended this was a routine medical situation. Which in most people's eyes it was. Should be in his, but that was Brooke down there, and while she was only doing what she probably did many times in her work, he didn't like being the recipient for some inexplicable reason. She was getting to him in the strangest ways, getting under his skin little by little.

Standing up, Brooke said, 'There's a towel in the bathroom cupboard and plenty of hot water if you want a shower while I get your gear. If you think you can manage by yourself, that is.'

'Can't be too hard.'

That could not be disappointment widening her eyes. Did she want to get into the shower with him? Hold him steady? When he had a wall to lean against? Did she want to wash his back? His gut tightened, quickly followed by his groin. *Steady, Danny boy. Don't rush things.* This was a rush? He wasn't going nearly as fast as earlier. That'd been whizz-bang, great sex all over in no time at all. Though the memories were vivid, and likely to remain so for a long time.

Stepping off the porch, Brooke said over her shoulder, 'Back in a minute. Make yourself at home.'

'Brooke…' Danny called softly.

She spun around to stare at him. 'Yes?'

'Thanks for helping me. You're a legend.' He faltered to a stop. So much for going slowly. Next thing he knew, she'd be using that to get to him even further.

'As if I wouldn't look out for you. Or anyone in the same situation.'

'It's what you do. I know that, but still…' He shrugged.

That's not disappointment beating in my chest because you accepted my comment as though it was nothing out of the ordinary.

If only she knew. He didn't want her to

know. Not yet, when he was happy enjoying her company without looking over his shoulder. Hard to believe they'd only met that morning. Everything could, most likely would, come to an abrupt end when she learned who he was. But that was not happening. Not today. Or tomorrow. Having some uninhibited fun with this wonderful woman was holding him back from opening up.

He *was* getting stirred up in a hurry. There was a lot of ground to cover before he could even let words like that enter his mind. Lots of ground.

'Go get out of those wet clothes, will you?' Brooke sounded impatient.

Fair enough. His feet felt as though they were stuck to the deck. Even his bad knee felt heavier than it should. 'On my way.'

When I can move.

'You want a hand?'

'No, thanks.' Taking a tentative step, he reached the door, grateful his legs were obeying his messed-up mind. Removing his jacket, he slung it on a hook by the door and hobbled inside, where the warmth hit him, making his wet clothes cumbersome. His skin tingled as bumps rose. Where was the bathroom? Down the hall he found what he was looking for. Shucking his shirt, he tried to remove his jeans, but being wet they clung to his skin. Getting his injured knee out was going to be fun.

'Let me do that.' Brooke stood in the doorway.

'Thought you'd gone to get my gear.' His gaze dropped. His bag swung from her hand. 'Have I been that long getting absolutely nowhere?' All he'd done was enter the house and get half undressed. When had he become such a geriatric? She'd be thinking he was useless.

'It's not like I don't know my way around Mike's house.' Her laugh lifted his suddenly despondent spirits. 'Sit on the edge of the bath so I can roll your jeans off without hurting too much.'

'Anyone ever tell you you're bossy?'

'My sister does all the time. She's the oldest and thinks she still holds the boss card. It's been my life mission to show her she's wrong.'

Whip.

His leg was free with hardly a stab of pain.

'There. I'll leave you to get showered.' Standing up, Brooke glanced at him, and her smile wavered. 'Unless you need me.'

Don't look below my waist. I need you, all right. Nothing to do with getting warm and clean, and all to do with letting go and enjoy-

ing you and giving you something back for making me feel this way.

'Are you any good at washing backs?'

'I could be.' It wasn't a whisper, but neither did Brooke yell. 'Do you think that would be wise, given your—' Her gaze dropped, and her mouth opened, turned into a big smile. 'We have to be careful.'

'We'll manage.' While their minds were still working, but for how long was anyone's guess. His being that it would be many minutes.

Then Brooke went all serious on him. 'Are you sure? I'd hate to bump that knee.'

'Do I look uncertain?' he asked with a cheeky grin.

'I guess not.' Her fingers were already working at the buttons of her shirt. Then she stopped.

Another doubt coming up?

She crossed to turn the shower on. Then she got towels off a shelf. Finally she went back to stripping out of her clothes.

The room warmed up fast. Nothing to do with the steam beginning to rise from the shower. All to do with the sight unfolding before him. If he hadn't been hard before, he certainly was now. So much he barely felt his knee as he moved to the shower and stepped under the water, closing his eyes to take a moment to settle the pounding under his ribs.

Soft circling movements on his back. Brooke had slipped behind him as he let the water pummel his face. Her hands were firm yet gentle as she caressed him. So much for quieting his heart. She was winding him so tight he might burst apart. Turning carefully, Danny reached for Brooke and leaned in to kiss her. Ignoring the painful reminders to go easy coming from his knee, he leaned back enough to touch her breasts, leaned close and kissed them, drawing her nipple into his mouth to run his tongue over the tip.

Above him, Brooke gasped, and her hands dug into his backside to pull him closer. His arousal pressed hard against her stomach. He had to have her. If she was ready. He'd make her ready. When his finger found her need, she cried out. Then encased him in her hand, rubbing him hard, taking his breath away, turning him tighter than ever.

'Brooke,' he gasped against her breast. 'Slow down. I can't take much more. I want to make you come first.'

Using the shower wall as leverage, she lifted up and hooked her legs around his waist. 'Now, Danny. Right now,' she groaned by his ear. 'Please.'

Happy to oblige, he pushed up into her. Once, then again, and again, until she cried out and tightened around him. His heart belted against his ribs. His mind was blank apart from the heat and relief rushing through his body. His hands held Brooke's backside, feeling her quivering as she came and came. Then he lost all control and joined her in wonder.

CHAPTER SIX

BROOKE DRIED HER HAIR, staring at the smile on her lips. No way could she stop her mouth beaming. Her whole body was limp, happy, sated. Danny was one heck of a lover. He'd brought her to a peak in an instant and delivered on his promise fast and wonderfully.

They'd had sex that morning. Now they'd made love. It didn't mean they were in love, but what they'd shared was more than a rip-your-clothes-off-and-get-it-together act. There'd been a tenderness amidst the heat and speed of that moment that she couldn't describe other than she'd felt beyond wanted and free, beyond having fun to something deeper. Yeah, and she had ripped her clothes off.

Of course she was overreacting and jumping in too fast. A day ago she hadn't known Danny. Still didn't really. Like Danny who? Did it matter? Only if there was an ominous reason for him not saying. She could ask, but for once she didn't want to spoil what was going on between them. She wanted to enjoy the rest of the weekend and see where it led. That seemed perfect, and what could be better than perfect?

'Knock, knock. Did you mention ice in the freezer?' Danny stood lopsidedly, taking the pressure off his injured leg.

'I'll get it, and the casserole.'

'How many meals did your mother leave for you?'

'Plenty. She loves cooking. There's cake and some desserts too.' These days her mother tried to make up for the past hurt by doing lots of loving things for her. Brooke had finally explained to her how much her mother's approach to certain situations took away Brooke's control. Her mum had apologised profusely, and said she finally understood her daughter's stance. Brooke had forgiven her in an instant. Grudges were a waste of energy and, no matter what, she was her mother.

'I don't need those.' Danny rubbed his stomach. 'As tempting as they sound.'

'You like to keep fit?'

He nodded. 'I run a lot, though that's going to take a rest for a little while. I also work out at the gym. It's what I've always done. I see too many unhealthy people through work to want to give keeping fit a miss.'

'Know what you mean. Though I'm not a fitness addict, I do run and cycle.'

'It shows. You look good.'

She blushed, something that was happening too often today. 'Thanks.'

'You're not used to compliments.'

'Can't say I am.' There wasn't anyone to give them out. No one important, any rate. 'It's been a while,' she said in a strong voice. It might be true but she wasn't looking for sympathy. She probably shouldn't have said it, but it was just another effect Danny was having on her—she was talking too much. 'I'll get the ice while you find somewhere to make yourself comfortable.'

She all but danced out to the laundry where the freezer stood. This whole scenario was so bizarre it was funny. Interesting and exhilarating. Then she looked out of the window and her smile faded. Old Man Duggan's house was destroyed enough to suggest he probably wouldn't be moving back. It would take at least a year to clear away the wreckage and get planning permission for a new house, to draw up plans and have it built. He would likely end up in a retirement home, a place he'd often said he never wanted to go. Her heart broke for him.

She loved the old man. He was like a second granddad to her, hence calling him Old Man Duggan.

'Here you go,' she said, handing the ice to Danny, who'd claimed the couch to sit on with his legs up.

His knee was red and swollen, yet he wasn't having too much trouble moving it. 'It's not bad,' he affirmed. 'I'll strap it later.'

Winding the ice bag around Danny's knee, Brooke tried not to think too much about his firm muscles and how wonderful it'd felt wrapping her legs around his waist in the shower. It seemed she'd flipped a switch and her life was now exciting and fast filling with all sorts of possibilities. She hadn't realised just how much she was missing having a man in her life. She taped the bag in place.

'Hello? Where have you gone?' Danny tapped her shoulder. 'You have a habit of going off somewhere I can't follow.'

Brooke crossed to sit on a lounge chair. 'I don't mean to.' It wasn't something she usually did, but the more time she spent with Danny the more she was comparing her previous relationships and seeing him for the great guy she hoped he really was. She shook her head. 'I'm doing it again, aren't I?'

He laughed, apparently unfazed by her lack

of attention. 'No problem. It's not something I'm used to, that's all.'

'Used to women swooning at your knees, are you?' she said with a chuckle.

His laughter died away, and for a moment he said nothing. Until—'I like genuine women, and you certainly seem to be that. I can't believe we've only just met. I feel as though I've known you far longer.'

Talk about upfront—for once. 'The circumstances have been demanding and exceptional.'

The laughter returned. 'That explains it. Your normal first date is at a café for a coffee and muffin.'

Brooke relaxed. She didn't like it when he went all serious. 'More like a pub and a wine.'

'I'll take note of that.'

He was going to ask her out? On her thighs, her fingers were doing a little dance. Bring it on.

Danny fed more wood into the firebox, biting down on the sharp stab of pain from his knee. Time for more painkillers. Brooke was snoozing in her chair, the day having finally caught up with her.

They'd eaten dinner sitting here in the warm glow from the fire, and he'd cleaned up the kitchen afterwards despite Brooke saying he should take it easy. She didn't know him well enough to realise he wasn't one for sitting around even when injured, and today's injury was minor.

A little snore reached him and he wanted to run his hand over her silky hair, to feel her warmth on his skin, to be close. Danny returned to the couch. He should wake her and insist she go to bed, but it was great sitting here watching her. She was lovely. He was so sure of that he could almost feel the truth slipping off his tongue between them as he explained who he was and why he tried to downplay the past so hard. One day wasn't enough to be certain she would remain so accepting of who he presented himself to be.

It wasn't as though he was being dishonest. He *was* a medical intern who revelled in the work he did, because he liked to help people and because he enjoyed the medical puzzles that presented themselves with every patient. Yes, he'd been an avid sportsman and fitness freak. He'd also always been fascinated with medicine after listening to his grandfather tell him stories from his private practice. He'd revelled in his ability to outplay other golfing champions. He also enjoyed putting people back together both physically and mentally after they'd copped one of life's arrows.

In that way he was luckier than some. His

golf career had crashed and burned, and for a while it had been hard to get back on his feet and face the future. His family had rallied around him, giving him time and encouragement to get it right. His body had recovered quicker than his mind, but he'd made it because he did believe in himself, did understand he could do well in whatever field he chose to work in.

Medicine was interesting, exciting, and hard on the heart at times. Patients didn't always make it out of the front door of the hospital. That sucked. But it was unavoidable. He did his absolute best to be there for them and their families. He had no regrets about his career choice, and sometimes even admitted to himself that it might have been for the best he'd had to stop playing golf. He'd been getting too big for his boots. Hard not to when the television crews were always tracking him, when women were all but begging to be his next bed partner. It was his family who'd kept him mostly on track. He owed them for that.

If only he could find a woman who'd be the perfect match, who'd support him without looking for what she wanted from his past, his future, his bank account. Sure, sharing a home and family was his dream, but could he please have that without all the nonsense?

His gaze never left Brooke for a moment. Her breasts rose and fell gently under her cream angora jersey. Her hair fell across one side of her face, highlighting her fine bone structure. She was lovely, heart-warming. There'd been concern in her eyes as she'd tried to rescue her neighbour, and when she'd dug his foot out of the mud so he didn't have to yank it free, causing added pain. Not that he wouldn't have done so if he'd been on his own.

Yes, he liked Brooke Williams a lot already. Already, as in he hoped to spend more time with her. She hadn't backed away when he'd said he'd remember she liked going to the pub for a wine. Nor had she leapt in and demanded an instant invitation. This was a special time for him, and he was afraid to ruin it by bringing in the past. Then again, he might wreck any chance with her if he didn't fill her in soon.

'You're staring,' Brooke murmured as she straightened her legs out from under that firm, sensual backside he'd held in the shower. 'How long have I been asleep?'

'About thirty minutes.'

She glanced at the wall clock. 'Might as well hit the sack and get some real sleep. Do you want a bed or are you happy staying on the couch?'

'I'd prefer a bed, so I'll head over to Mike's.'

'There are beds made up here.' She paused, looked at him with a hint of a smile. 'Or you could share mine and we'd be warm together.'

Danny was already getting warmer and he hadn't moved. The idea of curling up with Brooke was perfect, making him smile like a kid in the lolly shop. 'Yes, please.'

She blinked and stared at him some more. 'You're sure?'

What had brought on that sudden doubt?

'If you're changing your mind I won't get upset.'

'Not at all. This is quite unexpected, that's all. I don't usually get so close to a man I've only just met.'

Somehow that didn't surprise him, despite how fast they'd torn each other's clothes off that morning. She seemed too contained to be anything but cautious with a stranger. Yet she hadn't been like that with him, which made him soften more towards her and want to protect her. Could be that she didn't think of him as a stranger.

'You can still say no to sharing your bed.'

Her hair flicked around her head as she shook it. 'I'm looking forward to it. Come on, let's move. Unless it's too early for you. It's barely past nine.'

'Feels more like midnight. It's been a day

and a half for real.' He stood up slowly, favouring his knee. Brooke's fingers had been so gentle as she'd wound the crepe bandage round his leg he'd almost enjoyed the process.

Stripping down to his underpants, Danny slid between the sheets and studied the photos on the wall. One was of an older couple and Brooke with another woman. The sister she'd mentioned? And her parents? In another a much younger Brooke was laughing at the camera as she held up a large fish, which he didn't recognise, with both hands. Brooke's face was split with a grin and laughter lit up her eyes. He'd long forgotten what it was like to feel so relaxed; he was always wary and distrustful of people's motives. Strange he didn't feel that way with Brooke. He almost had to remind himself to be careful.

She entered the bedroom, dressed in winter pyjamas that wouldn't have won a glamour award and made her look soft and cuddly. 'That's a snapper.' She tapped the photo he'd been looking at. 'A big one. Eighteen kilos.'

'You wound it in?' That would take some effort if it fought.

'Every metre of the way. I wasn't letting Dad take over, though he was itching to. Mostly afraid I'd lose it. Best fish I've ever eaten.' Her face reflected the same laughing smile she'd worn in the photo.

'I've never done much fishing. I might have to give it a go while I'm here.'

Slipping in beside him, she rolled onto her side and looked at him with interest. And puzzlement.

He could see she was tossing up questions, wondering which to ask. Instead of cutting her off, he held his breath and waited, hoping it wasn't going to be something he'd have to dodge.

'How long do you think you'll be in the country?'

So far he was safe. 'I'm here until the end of the year, when I'll return to the hospital in Melbourne where I did my junior training.'

'Is that where you want to specialise?'

'It seems appropriate to carry on there. I'm not sure where I'll go once I'm qualified. It'll depend on where I get a job.'

'You might come back to New Zealand.'

'I might.' At the moment he didn't want to leave at all. Didn't want to go to Nelson yet either. Being with Brooke was tantamount to being in paradise.

'I'm guessing since you haven't done much fishing you haven't lived on the coast?' She was clever. That was a tactful way of asking where he grew up.

'I grew up in Ballarat, well north of Melbourne.' Under the sheet, Danny's hands clenched. He was being honest. Too damned honest. What was he thinking? Getting to know Brooke better didn't have to mean talking about himself. Not yet. Not while he could relax and have some fun without waiting for the truth to hit.

'It's okay. I won't tell anyone,' she teased with a mix of fun and concern in her voice. 'Your secret's safe with me.'

Loosening his fingers, he reached for her and pulled her into a body-length hug, an arm over her waist, thighs pressing against hers, shins feeling her toes, chest to breasts.

It wasn't a secret as such, more a way of having some freedom for a little while. He definitely would talk to her about his past one day—if they saw more of each other once he left here. But not today. Nor tomorrow. The thought of seeing recognition dawn in those beautiful eyes made him tired and sad. There was a chance she wouldn't have a clue who Daniel Collins was, but past experience told him that it wouldn't take long for her to look him up. He'd tell her everything, but reality was clearer when seen in the media. Damn, he

was bitter. How about giving Brooke a chance?
It was early days, and there was a possibility
what they'd started could come to more.

'Your turn to spacewalk?' Her voice was
muffled by his neck, where she'd placed a light
kiss.

'I'm right here with you.' He reached across
to switch off the light and snuggled down with
Brooke, ignoring the painful twinges in his
knee. Nothing was going to get in the way
of this moment. Or the next ones. His mouth
sought hers, covered her lips, and he began
kissing her, slowly, tenderly. A kiss like no
other. Brooke did that to him. She'd changed
him already. Was this love at first sight? No, he
wasn't in love. But he might be falling into it.

His kiss deepened, and Brooke responded
with an intensity of her own.

And he fell a little bit more.

It might have been too cloudy to view the
stars above as Brooke had suggested, but right
now there were stars aplenty in his head. And
his heart.

'In my mind I keep hearing Lloyd calling for
Jean.' Brooke placed a plate of toast on the
table. 'I'm going to look for some photos for
him this morning.'

'Don't you think it'll be too dangerous to go inside that house?'

'I'm hoping nothing much has changed overnight. If there's more damage I'll rethink the idea, but at the moment I'm going in.' She'd be careful—and fast. She knew where there'd likely be some framed pictures. 'It'll be a snatch and grab.'

Danny said, 'I'm not missing out on the raid.' He wasn't smiling or laughing; he was serious. He was that kind of guy.

He hadn't baulked about helping her yesterday and, apart from querying the safety factor, he hadn't now. In her mind that made him a keeper. First tick to becoming one anyway. 'Thanks,' she said. 'But only if you're not going to mess with that knee.'

'The knee's good.'

'So that wasn't a groan of pain when you got out of bed?'

'You would prefer me to be a wimp?' he asked with a little smile tipping those erotic lips upward.

'Nothing wimpy about you so far.' Danny had been hard as rock when they'd made love during the night. A generous lover, he gave more than he took, making certain she was ready and willing. Except he'd have had to be deaf, blind and dumb not to know when she was ready, all but begging for release.

'Are you going to start clearing your back-yard today?'

Blowing on her coffee, she watched as he slathered butter on his toast, remembering those fingers on her body. She blew harder on the coffee. 'Maybe.'

His head came up and he locked his gaze on her. 'Maybe?'

Her cheeks heated. 'We'll see.'

We might have better things to do.

When Brooke went outside she heard a dig-ger working on the road. 'Sounds like the road might be open later today,' she called to Danny.

'I'm quite happy being stuck here for an-other day.'

'You're due at the ED tomorrow afternoon.'

'I've got a good excuse not to be. I don't usu-ally try to get out of turning up for work. It's only that I'm so relaxed I don't want to leave.'

She knew what he meant. For her, it wouldn't be quite the same when he did head away. 'Do you think you'll be able to drive with your bung knee?'

'It's improving all the time, and tomorrow's a while away. I'll see how it is then.'

'I can drive you to Nelson if need be.' A

three-hour round trip wouldn't be a problem, especially spending half of it with Danny.

'Thanks for the offer, but hopefully I'll be fine because I'll need my car. It's also got all my worldly goods in the back. As in clothes, books and laptop.'

Which would be easy enough to transfer to her car, but Danny seemed determined to drive himself. She doubted he'd do it if his knee wasn't up to it, though he might not be insured if he had an accident. His fault or not.

'Insurance?'

He looked away. 'I can cover it.'

She'd mentioned insurance, nothing about his wealth or lack of. Her eyes cruised over his wet weather jacket and trendy trekking trousers, down to a pair of fashionable walking shoes. No lack of funds there. A glance next door at the latest model four-wheel drive vehicle parked outside Mike's house backed her thoughts. It made her second-hand wagon look worn-out when it was barely five years old. It was solid, reliable and went like a cut cat when she was out on the open road. What more did she need?

'I'll get the gas bottle while I'm out here.' She'd never got around to it yesterday, what with everything else going on.

'Let me do that.' Danny was already striding unevenly for the shed.

The tank was heavy, and weight was the last thing he needed to put on his knee. About to say so, she stopped. He wouldn't like her insisting she carry the tank. He seemed to be a man who helped women and wouldn't step back for any reason. She wasn't ready to upset him by demanding he back off when they were getting along so well. Besides, it was great having a man taking care of her. She could get to like it. She wouldn't mention her aching bruises. He might get too protective.

'Here's the key.'

Danny was back within minutes, the tank swinging from his hand as if it was light as a football. 'I'll put it on the porch, shall I?'

'That's fine.' At least she wouldn't have to go out to the shed in the dark now if it ran out during the evening.

Brooke headed for the house next door, or what was left of it. Without the rain and wind buffeting her, she could see how bad the damage was. The boulder that hit the back wall was wedged firmly between the doors to the kitchen and laundry. The wall where she'd been going to climb through the window now leaned at a precarious angle.

'Looks worse today.'

'It does.'

She jumped. She hadn't heard Danny coming closer.

He laid his hand over her shoulder to draw her near. 'Sorry. I should've been puddle jumping and then you'd have heard me approaching.'

For a brief moment she snuggled closer, enjoying his strength. It felt solid, reliable, with a sense of safety and comfort. 'Let's check the front door, see if there's any change.'

'If it's too dangerous, please don't go in.' Danny's arm was still around her shoulders, keeping her with him as they made their way through the debris. 'I understand it's important to you to find some photos, but your safety has to come first.'

Her heart melted a little bit. Whether he was being friendly and caring or he really was concerned for her, it didn't matter. It sounded great and it was something she'd needed to hear from a special person for a while. Danny mightn't be her man, or so special she couldn't live without him, but he was getting further and further under her skin every minute. Waving him off tomorrow would be a wrench. If only she could go ask the digger driver to stop what he was doing and go move another slip further out. But the day would still arrive when Danny left.

'Lloyd wouldn't forgive me if I got hurt trying to help him.'

'No, he wouldn't.' Danny hugged her before going around to the front of the house. As though they were both used to being together and getting on with whatever called.

Joining him, hands on hips, she stared at the gap they'd come through yesterday. 'This doesn't appear to have moved at all.'

Stepping onto the wobbly deck, Danny peered inside. 'Looks pretty much the same at it was.' He moved inside.

Brooke followed. 'You don't need to be in here. I know what I'm looking for.'

She worked her way over the muddy floor. The bookcase had toppled over so books lay on the floor, ruined. As were the first three photos she found. Her heart sinking, she kept searching. 'Yes—' she sighed as she lifted a frame from the couch '—Jean and Lloyd on the beach.'

'Here's another one.' Danny passed her a silver frame.

'Their last wedding anniversary, on a cruise down Australia's east coast.' The building creaked, sending shivers down Brooke's spine. 'Two's good. Let's get out of here.'

'What about clothes for Lloyd?'

Along the hallway, one wall was on a slant and a panel ceiling had fallen to the floor. 'His bedroom's past that buckled patch of wall. Think I'll give it a miss.'

'Wise decision.' Danny turned for the front door. 'Let's get out of here.' So he wasn't comfortable either.

'Next stop the bike shed. We'll see how that digger driver's getting on.' It was always good to know what the options were. One never knew what might happen, especially after the storm they'd been through. The hills were unstable, and the roads would have been undermined by all the water still pouring down. As much as she'd like Danny stuck here a few more days, getting caught in another slip wasn't an option they needed to deal with.

Slip, slide, all the way to the shed, and Brooke was out of breath as she struggled to stay on her feet. 'Who needs to go for a run when I can walk around the yard all day?'

Danny grimaced as he lifted his injured leg free of a puddle of mud. 'Should've worn those boots you offered.'

'I do know what I'm talking about sometimes.'

'I'll remember that,' he muttered as he raised the shed door for her.

Brooke drove the bike forward and waited for Danny to climb on behind and wrap an arm around her. They had a routine going. Were they falling into sync too fast? Possibly, but it was fun.

Rounding the corner, Brooke brought the bike to a halt well away from the slip, where a digger was moving bucket-loads of clay and rotten rock onto one of two trucks lined up.

A driver spotted them and sauntered over. 'Morning. Bit of a mess, eh?'

'Worst storm I've been in out here. My family has a bach in the next bay,' Brooke explained. 'What's it like before here?'

'Three massive slips, which we've managed to clear enough so essential traffic can get through. There's also metre-deep mud covering about half a kilometre of road that's being cleared as we speak. A narrow track was made for us to get through, but you wouldn't want to be taking a car along there yet.'

Danny asked, 'How long before the road's passable? I'm hoping to get out first thing tomorrow.'

'You'll be right, mate. The guys reckon they'll have it cleared by tonight.'

Brooke swallowed her disappointment. Danny had to leave. But for once she wanted to be difficult and keep him here. *Toughen up, woman.* Danny had a life. So did she. If he was as keen as she was, they'd make it work. Only not for the next few days.

They got back on the bike and returned to the house.

'Is there a trailer we can use to cart away those branches?' Danny asked as he gazed around the yard. 'Or should we stack them somewhere for firewood?' He started wandering towards a broken tree, totally disregarding his knee.

'You're okay with the pain level?' It was as though he'd learned to cope with pain before.

'It's not bad.' He lifted a heavy clay pot that had rolled down from the shed and winced as he straightened.

'How come you already had painkillers in your bag?' she asked.

Lowering the pot back on the stand it had fallen off, he looked around then over to her. 'I injured my shoulder years ago and sometimes I get a few niggles, especially when I've been sitting too long.'

'How did you do that?'

'Slammed into some concrete. Now, what do you think? Stack the bigger pieces by the woodshed, or put them on the trailer?'

'Firewood's always useful.' She got it. Shut

up and don't ask any more. Well, tough. 'Did you fall off a bike or something?'

'No, I dived into a swimming pool badly.' He didn't even glance her way. 'Now, are we doing this?'

'Yes,' she snapped. Why he didn't like talking about something that didn't sound like a major catastrophe was beyond her. More than annoying. More like infuriating. Was she expecting too much too soon? Could be. A deep breath didn't help her relax any, so she grabbed a shovel to dig mud away from the trees.

He banged a heavy branch against the shed. How he managed to drag it through the mud without putting pressure on his knee was beyond her. But he was a man, and from her experience they did like to prove they weren't wimps. From what she'd seen so far, Danny got on with whatever had to be done, and didn't try to find an excuse not to do so. Her kind of man—if he didn't keep major secrets from her in the future.

Spinning around, Brooke stomped over to another fallen branch, trying to ignore the sudden thumping going on in her chest. *Her kind of man.* What planet was she on? She didn't have a type. Sure she did. Strong and gentle, serious and fun, kind and sexy. Definitely sexy and generous in that department.

Tick, tick, tick, tick, tick, tick and tick. So—her kind of man.

How could she think so when she was worried about his caution? Because her pulse had raced pretty much all the time since she'd met him and went crazy when they kissed and made love. Because she felt safe around him. Because…because of a hundred reasons. *Scary.* Last time she'd fallen in love it had all turned to trouble, so much so that she had come to enjoy living on her own, being in charge of her choices about everything. That was something she'd find hard to give up.

Getting ahead of yourself, Brooke.

She sure was. It was exciting and frightening. And possibly a total mistake. How could she trust Danny when she had this sense deep inside of being kept in the dark? He was probably having fun and wasn't thinking past when he drove out of here tomorrow morning. He certainly wasn't talking non-stop about his past or even his future, which most guys she'd dated recently seemed to do. They came with an agenda that included saying what they wanted for the future and why couldn't she see they were right for her. Was she getting too used to doing things her way now? Was she looking for trouble because she couldn't let go the past hurts?

She did want to find a man to love and make a life with. But, whoever it was, he would have to accept she wasn't a pushover. Glancing at Danny, air stalled in her lungs. So far he was looking better and better by the hour. She hadn't had such amazing sex in forever, or enjoyed sitting around talking or not, sharing a meal and a whisky so much. She was relaxed with him, wasn't looking for trouble. He was something else.

'Coffee and muffins on the front deck. Who'd have believed it after yesterday?' Danny stretched his legs out as he looked over the lawn, running down to the beach where driftwood had piled up haphazardly. This place was magical, despite showing how rough it could be. There had been beauty in the storm too, though it'd been worrying once the hills started sliding down.

'A normal day in paradise,' Brooke said. 'In summer we get severe storms as well as stunning hot, cloudless and windless weeks on end.'

'I hope to be here for some of those.' Sitting on this particular deck with this particular woman.

'Thought you said you'd be back in Melbourne by then.'

She didn't miss a trick. 'I might be able to drag out my start date over there for a little longer.' If he put in for a change now. To be fair, which he usually tried to be, hospitals were always crying out for staff over the summer break, and him wanting to have an extra couple of weeks off before turning up might be a problem. If he and Brooke were still getting along as well as they'd started out, he'd look into it. 'Do you spend Christmas and New Year here?'

'I come back and forth, depending on my roster. Next summer I'm due to have two weeks off since I've stood in for everyone else the last two years.'

Why didn't that surprise him? From what he'd seen so far, she was kind and generous.

'Your whole family comes here?'

'It depends on what Saskia has on, and who she's with, but Mum and Dad are always here. No exception. They spend more time together these days, now Dad's no longer working. Does your family do joint holidays?'

'Not often now. My parents like to go over to Wales to stay with Mum's sister. Mum's Welsh and met Dad when he was over there on a golfing trip.' Oh, oh. Mentioning golf not clever. Move on. Fast. 'My brother's married and lives in Vancouver.'

'So golf is a family pastime?'

Serve him right for mentioning how he'd first done in his knee. Golf and Daniel Collins were synonymous. All Brooke had to do was look up either and she'd learn all about him. No, not all. There was the part of him that thrived on becoming a doctor, and another that wanted nothing more than to fall in love with a woman who accepted him for all his faults and wealth without making demands on him to change. That was not recorded on any website or in any interview.

'Dad and I play the occasional game.'

'Who's the best?' Brooke was grinning. She really had no idea. Thank goodness.

'Me, of course.'

'You'd say that anyway, wouldn't you?'

'Yep.' Because it was true, and because when she did find out she couldn't say he'd lied. 'You ever given golf a go?'

Laughter filled the quiet. 'Once. I was hopeless. I have more chance of winning millions in a lottery than coordinating a club with a ball, let alone getting the ball in the air.'

'Not many people can on their first attempt.' He'd been lucky. He really had. 'If you had those millions, what would you do with them?' He was on a roll, wanting to learn how she might react to his situation.

'Get a newer car and change my carpet.' She grinned. 'Naturally I'd share with my family. Otherwise—' she shrugged '—I really have no idea. Of course I'd spend more, have some fun, but it seems almost more of a problem than anything else. Having that much money would be a responsibility. I'd want to give some to charities, but choosing which ones wouldn't be as easy as a stab in the dark.' She sounded completely genuine.

Danny didn't know whether to be impressed or sceptical. He'd heard it all before, yet knew how, when people did have access to so much money, they changed. He had. No denying it. He'd become arrogant and cocky, until the accident that had changed everything. It had taken a while, but eventually he'd learned how lucky he'd been and to make the most of what he'd got.

'A lot of people who win big lose it all within a very short time.'

'So I've heard. What would you do?'

'Employ my brother, who's an accountant-cum-business CEO, to invest it and oversee any donations I made.' That was exactly what he *had* done. Cooper was the financial brains in his family.

'I might buy a ticket when I get out of here.

Maybe the luck of not getting hit by that land-slide will continue.'

'Go for it. Who knows? You might get lucky and I can introduce you to my brother.' *Yikes.* His tongue really did run away with him around Brooke. He was talking so much about himself it was ridiculous. Because he felt close to her. Very close. Too close? So what if he did? He liked her. A lot. *And* he wanted to follow through. He really did. A knot formed in his gut. The standard warning sign for him. *Don't trust her so readily. Wait, be patient, learn more about her.*

But he'd been waiting for Brooke for years. Now he'd found her, he didn't want to let her go. He was already halfway to falling for this beautiful woman and he hadn't checked her out enough. *Let go of the past and move on with the future.* His new motto? Or a damned stu-pid idea? The knot wasn't getting any tighter, if anything it was loosening. A sign he was on the right track? He hoped so. More than that, he was prepared to find out. Slowly, care-fully, but definitely, he wanted to get closer to Brooke.

Brooke tapped his foot with hers. 'You've gone quiet again. You got something to hide?' There was concern behind her smile. Had someone hurt her by hiding the truth?

If that was so, he didn't want to be the one who repeated it. But, even feeling ready to make some attempt to let go of what had held him in place for so long, he couldn't quite bring himself to act on his feelings for her. They were too new, too raw, and might turn out to be a complete mistake.

'Sorry, it's a bad habit.' That was true. 'I've done it for a while now.'

'Why?'

He'd set himself up for that. 'I'm not good at sharing myself.' Also true. She was going to ask why again. He could feel it. 'You're very open with people, aren't you?'

'Up to a point. But I have been hurt more than once by people hiding important things from me and the idea of it happening again gives me chills.'

'You're honest.' He wasn't. He was being dishonest in what he wasn't saying. He could hurt her badly.

So, tell her the truth.

If only he could guarantee she wouldn't turn out like the others. What if she didn't? He just wanted these two days with her, happy and relaxed, before putting his heart on the line. There was a real possibility of losing her trust if her reaction was what he wanted, but he wasn't quite ready. It was too soon.

Standing up abruptly, he held out his hand for her mug. 'Want another coffee?' He didn't, but he'd have one if it meant the end of this particular conversation.

Brooke shook her head. 'Sit down. I won't eat you. Or demand answers to questions that obviously bother you.' She watched as he slowly placed his butt back on the outdoor chair. 'We hadn't met until a little more than thirty hours ago and we seem to have got on faster than I've experienced with other men. Let's leave it at that for now.'

For now meant hope for the future, didn't it? He reached for her hand and wound his fingers between hers. He wanted to tell her she was special. The words were there, on the tip of his tongue, pushing to get out. Breathe in, one two three. He couldn't do it. Not yet.

'Despite the storm, I'm glad I came to the bay for the weekend.'

'So am I.'

His fingers tightened briefly. Brooke was wonderful.

Patience, man. You're going like a bat out of hell over this, and the result is likely to be you'll scare the pants off her and you'll never see her again.

He had to take his time so no nasty surprises arose. So he could tell her everything that'd made him who he was. Mostly so he could enjoy the whole journey, not stop half-way along. Except he knew better. The past always caught up.

Huffing out his disappointment, he asked, 'I'm serious about another coffee. I could do warming up.'

'I know another way to fix that.' Now it was Brooke's fingers tightening their grip around his. Her eyes had widened and were filled with an invitation.

He kissed her knuckles. 'Sounds more than good to me.' Standing, he pulled her up against him and held her close as he kissed her. Deep and filled with longing. A kiss meant to tell her how he was feeling about her. A kiss to replace the words he couldn't put out there.

A shiver tripped up Brooke's spine. Danny kissed like the devil. He brought her awake in an instant, tightening all of her body so it was crying for release. His kisses were temptation on lips. They didn't take away her confusion about letting go her fear of being duped again. If those nearest and dearest could hurt her by not being open and honest then what was to say Danny couldn't? He'd dodged questions non-stop over the hours they'd been together.

His mouth left hers. 'Brooke? Are you all right?'

Yikes. She'd been doing a Danny, losing focus. What was more, she'd done it when his kisses were sensational. Was she rushing this? Probably. And enjoying it.

Stretching up on tiptoe, she whispered, 'I'm fine. Very distracted at the moment. By you,' she added in case he backed off, feeling unwanted.

'You're sure?' He was aware of her feelings. She'd never been good at hiding them.

'Very. Kiss me again,' she begged. She'd given in to these new feelings too easily, so she was going to make the most of them.

His reply was to place his mouth over hers and return to making her toes tingle, her skin lift and her heart dance. As simple as that. As complicated as that. She'd go with simple for now, drop all the questions threatening to return and upset the moment. Pushing her tongue into his mouth, she tasted him, absorbed his heat, breathed in the outdoorsy male air about him and gave her mind over to desire and pleasure.

As they lay entwined under her bedcovers, regaining their breath, Brooke heard a knock on the back door. 'Who can that be?' she said as she scrambled upright and grabbed her jeans. 'As far as I know, we're the only ones in the bay.'

Danny got out of bed too and began dressing. 'I'll come with you. Could be someone needs medical help and have heard you're here.'

When Brooke opened the door the truck driver from earlier stood on the porch with his hand raised, about to knock again. 'Howdy. Is the man who mentioned trying to get out here?'

'He is. Danny, someone to see you.' She smiled to herself. Didn't they sound like a regular couple?

'I'm Connor, by the way.'

'What's up?' Danny stepped out onto the porch.

'You were saying you had to get out tomorrow for work.'

'That's right.'

'Seems I was wrong about the road being open by then. It's likely to be two or three days before people will be allowed out, except for emergencies.'

Danny grimaced. 'Not much I can do about that. I'll try the water taxi.'

'Hang on,' Connor said. 'We have a truck going out to Blenheim to collect some gear required for the digger. The driver is happy to escort you as far as Picton. Without an escort you aren't allowed to go. It's too dangerous. They're not letting anyone else out. You also can't go the other way. That will be closed for a week at least.'

'When's the truck leaving?' Brooke could feel her heart beginning to speed up. Was her time with Danny up already?

'As soon as Danny's ready. We need the gear urgently.'

Danny looked from Connor to Brooke and shrugged. 'I'll go and throw my bag in the car.' He looked sad.

As sad as she suddenly felt. She would miss him, even if she could expect to see him in the ED next week. It wouldn't be the same with doctors, nurses and patients all around them. They'd basically been alone and she'd loved it. It seemed the storm had brought them together, and in a roundabout way was now pulling them apart.

'That's a yes then,' Connor said with a grin. 'I'll go tell Geo to wait for you. He'll explain what you've got to do.'

'Basically stick to his tail,' Danny said with a weak smile as he rubbed his shoulder against hers.

He didn't want to go. She'd swear it. Lifting

her shoulder up and back down, she acknowledged his touch.

Connor stepped off the porch, then paused. 'I'm hearing you two saved Lloyd.'

'We got him out of the house and gave him medical attention until the chopper arrived,' Brooke said, nodding. 'Have you heard how he's doing?'

'He's had surgery and been put back together. That's all I know. But the whole community is grateful you were here, or who knows when he'd have been found, or if he'd have survived his injuries.'

'You couldn't have stopped Brooke getting in to him. She was a woman on a mission.' Danny looked at her, admiration obvious in his eyes.

'You weren't so bad yourself,' she said quietly. Connor probably thought this was gag material.

'Right, see you shortly.' Connor strode away.

She said to Danny, 'I suspect they're helping you because we helped Lloyd. He's adored around the area.'

'It's good of them.' Danny took her shoulders and turned her so she was looking up at him. 'This has been very special, Brooke. I can't believe what's happening between us. Thank you for being...you.'

She sniffed. A flick of her hand over her eyes. 'It has.' She swallowed hard. 'I'll see you at work.' Not the same, but better than nothing.

'I hope so.'

That was it? He wasn't suggesting they get together in any other capacity? Her heart sank. She had no right to get upset. It had been a short acquaintance. He'd said the loveliest things, but she must've read too much into them.

You could ask him to meet up at the pub or go for a meal next weekend. And be turned down? *Nothing to lose except your pride, and that was used to taking a knock in the past.*

'Danny...'

'I'd better go. I got the feeling these guys are in a hurry to get to town.' He started to lean forwards, as if about to kiss her. Then he stopped, stepped back, rubbed a hand over his face. 'Take care.'

She grabbed him, placed her mouth on his and kissed him. Not softly. Not lightly. But hard and full of the passion that had simmered from the first time he'd helped her up out of the mud. A kiss that was a message—*I'm available if you want more time with me.* Pulling back, she told him, 'Be careful out there.' She spun around to head inside. Watching him walk away wasn't an option. It was too hard when she longed to hug him, kiss him again, tell him he was more than a two-day fling.

Thankfully her brain was running this, or her heart might have shouted out something like *I care about you and want to be with you*, and that would have been a deal-breaker for sure.

'Brooke, wait.'

Her breath stuck in her chest, like a stab of pain. What had he forgotten? Turning slowly, she stepped back onto the porch.

Danny had his phone in his hand. 'I don't have your number.'

The breath whooshed out as relief took hold. He wanted to keep in touch. It was a start.

He stood in front of her, an expectant look on his gorgeous face. 'Brooke?'

She rattled it off. 'Send me a text so I get yours.'

'Will do.' Leaning in, he brushed those gorgeous lips over hers. 'We're not done, Brooke.'

Returning his kiss with one of her own, she smiled beneath his lips. They weren't finished. Stepping back, because he did have to go, she asked, 'By the way, Danny who?'

He took a deep breath, held it a moment, then said quietly, 'Danny Collins.'

'Thanks.' No problem with that. Or was there? He had hesitated. No doubt she was looking for trouble. 'Let me know how you're settling in to Nelson, will you?'

I really want to hear from you.

Reaching for her hand, Danny looked right into her eyes. 'Brooke, if you're back by then, would you like to go out for a meal on Friday night?'

'I should be and I'd love to.' No thinking required. It was exactly what she'd love to do with Danny. A real date with a man who had her heart pounding and her brain wondering if she'd found the one.

'I'll call and let you know what time I'll pick you up when I'm clearer on what's happening with the job.' He kissed her again, a kiss that went right through her and touched her heart. 'See you later.'

And he was gone.

CHAPTER SEVEN

'DANNY, YOU TAKE THAT,' Gayle, the head of the ED, called over the blaring sound of the emergency bell ringing from the ambulance bay.

'Onto it.' Striding purposefully through the emergency department, Danny was quickly joined by Sarah, a nurse, pushing the resus trolley. 'Wonder what's going on,' he said.

'Cardiac arrest or seizure?' Sarah said.

'Bleed out,' Brooke told them even before they'd reached the ambulance to find a man lying on a stretcher on the floor of the parking bay. 'Cardiac arrest.' She was doing compressions while her offsider prepared the defibrillator.

At the sight of Brooke, Danny's eyes widened. She was meant to still be on leave. Kneeling beside the patient, he surveyed what injuries were apparent. 'Fill me in.'

'Stand back,' the other paramedic called.

The man jerked as the electric current hit him. The line remained flat.

Brooke continued with the compressions, totally focused. 'Brett Gibbons, thirty-seven, trauma from being struck by a truck as he tried to cross a road. Multiple fractures, internal injuries, head trauma.'

Anyone would be happy to have Brooke at their side when their life was in jeopardy, Danny thought. Including him.

'Where are we at with the bleeding?' There were swabs on most exposed parts of Brett's body, soaked through and still oozing.

'It's slowing, suggesting there's not much to come.' Brooke was breathing hard. Compressions were tough work.

The defib beeped. 'Stand back.'

Another jolt, another flat line.

And again. The fourth electric current was coming up and Danny held his breath.

Ping. The line moved up, down. Up, down. Not high, but it meant life. The heart had started. They'd been running out of time. Much longer and the man would be pronounced DOA.

'All hands to the stretcher,' Danny demanded.

Brooke already held one corner. Damn but she was smooth—and fast. And, in that green and black uniform, every bit as sexy as he'd dreamt all week.

'On the count,' Danny said. 'One, two, three.'

He, Sarah, Brooke and another nurse carefully lifted the stretcher onto the trolley and started back into the ED, the other paramedic following with the ambulance ECG still attached to their patient at her side.

'Emergency bed,' he said, though everyone would know that. This man needed the highest standard of care the department had. He wasn't out of trouble by a long shot. His heart rate was erratic and slow. He needed blood fast. Another cardiac arrest was very likely. That was only the beginning. There'd be sutures, X-rays, surgeons putting him back together, to think of a few.

Danny instructed the staff. 'Courtney, call for blood, three litres to start with. Hugo, let Radiology know we need them here with the portable unit. Sarah, start checking those bleeds.' He turned to Brooke. 'Tell me everything you've found.'

'Fractures in left femur and lower leg, right femur, and the left arm appears to have fractures.' Brooke turned a tight face towards him. 'There's swelling in the upper abdomen, and ribs are possibly broken. There's also a soft area at the front of his skull.'

The sorrow in her eyes for this man made Danny want to reach out with a very big hug. Instead he started on a thorough examination of Brett, speaking into the microphone attached to his tunic.

The ECG monitor was swapped over to the hospital one, leaving Brooke and the other paramedic free to leave, but she remained, standing to the side, watching everything he did.

A shrill sound filled the room. 'Flat line,' Sarah called.

Here we go again.

Danny began compressions while the defibrillator charged.

'Stand back.' Sarah pressed the button to send the shock into Brett's heart.

'Yes. Good result.' Danny wiped his brow with the back of his gloved hand. 'Get me the cardiology unit on the phone, Hugo.' This man needed a cardiologist right now. 'Where's that blood?'

'The lab's sending down interim red blood cell units and will take a sample for a cross match for later. They should be here within a few minutes,' Courtney informed him.

'Thanks.' Danny only hoped there was a later. At the moment this man was in a very dire situation, but he'd got this far, with help from Brooke no less.

'What do you want me doing?' Another doctor had arrived.

Where to start? 'Start suturing the severest lacerations so the blood loss doesn't continue after transfusion.'

'Here's Radiology,' Sarah reported.

They all got busy and when Danny finally straightened up his back ached, but they were getting somewhere. Brett was heading to Theatre for surgery on his liver and spleen, and a neurosurgeon would do what he could for the severe head wound causing a lack of consciousness. The fractures would have to wait until the more urgent problems were dealt with.

Brooke was long gone, back to her work of helping someone else. He smiled to himself as a picture of her in her uniform came to mind. Lovely even when fighting for someone else's life. He looked around.

An orderly stood ready to wheel their patient wherever the surgeons now examining Brett demanded.

Danny touched the man's hand even though he wouldn't feel it. 'Good luck, Brett.' Then he turned away. This was the difficult side of what he did. Not knowing if the patient would survive or not, or whether he'd be returning to his normal life in the future, took its toll. But he wouldn't change his job for anything else. Not even to return to being a top-ranking golfer. Being a doctor was about helping others, not looking after his own ego. There was a bit of that in the mix, Danny admitted as he threw his gloves in the bin. He was proud to be able to help people in pain, to make them well again, or at least comfortable. But there weren't any glaring lights and flashing cameras because it was more about the patient. He'd come a long way.

The next time Danny saw Brooke, she was wheeling in a little boy with his left arm in a sling. 'Danny, meet Thomas. He had a fight with the jungle gym at school.'

Danny crouched down so he was eye to eye with the little man. 'Looks like the jungle gym won, buddy. What have you done to yourself?'

'My arm's broken.' The kid sounded proud, not upset.

'You reckon? I'll have to have a look and make sure you're right.'

'I am.'

'We got a doctor in the making?' Danny straightened and asked the woman standing by the wheelchair, looking distressed and amused all in one.

'It's one of three occupations he has in mind

this week.' Thomas's mother shrugged. 'Better than last week's, which was to be a bank robber.'

Danny chuckled. 'Okay, Thomas, let's get you onto a bed first so I can have a look at your arm and check out the rest of you.'

'Nothing else hurts,' Thomas informed him, looking very serious. But that changed as he was helped onto the bed. He cried out, 'Stop it. I don't like that.' Tears spilled down his face.

'Does something else hurt besides your arm?' Danny noted Thomas wasn't putting any weight on his left side.

'He complained of pain around his hip when we first loaded him into the ambulance,' Brooke told him. 'Another boy who was there said Thomas landed on his hip and arm. There's swelling and bruising in that area. Otherwise nothing to report.' She handed the paperwork to Hugo, who'd just joined them.

Stepping away from the cubicle, Danny asked Brooke, 'You okay now? You looked shaken earlier.'

'I'm good. I get a little rattled once I've handed over a serious case. It's as if the tension lets go and I turn to jelly. Any news on how Brett's doing?'

'He's still in Theatre and will be there for quite a while.'

'I figured.' She sighed. 'Right, I'd better get going. We're having quite a busy day.'

'I thought you weren't back at work until Monday.'

'I was asked if I minded coming in, so I came back last night. Another AP's wife went into early labour. I could hardly say no.'

Of course she wouldn't. 'Still up for dinner?'

Brooke's face lit up. 'Try and stop me.'

'It's a date.' He headed back to Thomas, his feet skipping, his heart beating a happy rhythm.

Taking the washing out of the dryer, Brooke began folding it as she waited for Danny to turn up. He'd texted to say he was running late due to an emergency just as he was due to leave the department. She grinned. The joys of dating a doctor. When the text pinged on her phone and she'd seen his name, her stomach had dived. He was going to cancel, had changed his mind now he was back in town amongst more interesting people. Of course he hadn't. Danny wouldn't do that, would he? Her stomach had returned to normal. As normal as having a cage-load of butterflies flapping around in there could be. She couldn't understand this nervousness. He'd looked surprised, then pleased to see her in the ED so what was there to be edgy over? She'd missed him like crazy since he'd left the bay on Sunday—which was crazy in itself after such a short time together.

Was it because she really liked him and wanted to get closer? Probably. It couldn't be because she was falling for him.

It could be.

But there were all these doubts whenever he didn't tell her things about himself. Was she overreacting? It'd been a while since she'd felt this way about a man, long enough for her to start wondering if she'd always be on her own and that it wasn't such a bad state to be in because at least no one else was taking control of her day-to-day actions—and reactions. But she couldn't help thinking something was about to implode. That whatever Danny was keeping to himself might hurt her, or them.

Did she look all right in her black trousers and white frilly blouse? Crossing to the full-length mirror, she assessed her clothes. They fitted perfectly, accentuating all the right places. Black and white was ordinary. It was her go-to style because it didn't draw a lot of attention. Didn't she want to attract Danny's attention? Sure she did. Then she should have put on the ruby-coloured leather trousers and cream jersey. Her silver earrings swung when she turned her head this way and that. Her hair shone where it fell over her shoulders. The leather boots gave her some much-needed height for standing close to Danny.

The doorbell rang. It was too late to make changes. If he wasn't impressed then too bad. She was in control of herself, right? Yes, right...

Pulling the door wide, her heart lurched at the stunning sight on her front step. Danny was wearing a tan leather jacket, an open-necked white shirt and black trousers. Simple, and perfect. She could remember the body underneath, could feel his warmth against her skin.

'Hey,' she managed around the lump blocking her throat. How had she managed to get this man to even look at her, let alone want to take her out for a meal?

'Brooke, you look wonderful.' He stood watching her.

Managing not to say *You think?*, she smiled and felt goofy, as if his compliment was beyond amazing. 'Thanks.' When he said nothing else, she burbled on. 'Do you want to come in? Or should we get going?' It was nearly eight and her stomach had been crying out for food. Earlier her appetite had disappeared when Danny sent her hormones into a spin in the emergency department. Baggy scrubs weren't sexy, but picturing the fit body inside them was.

He nodded. 'Let's go eat.'

The fluttering slowed. This wasn't the Danny she'd spent time with last weekend. That Danny had held her hand at every opportunity, had smiled a lot. Was he regretting his dinner invitation? She thought about her unusually tidy bedroom, the bedcovers straightened and the pillows all fluffy. Her clothes might be ordinary but underneath she wore the sexiest G-string and bra she'd been able to buy when she'd got back to town late yesterday. She could have been wasting her time.

'Where are we going?'

'Do you know the Dock?'

Everyone talked about it. 'I haven't been there, but I've driven past numerous times.' It was small and supposedly quiet, sitting over the water on the edge of Nelson Harbour. 'This is going to be a treat.' She slipped into her vinyl jacket and zipped up the front.

'I hope so. It was recommended by one of the specialists at the hospital. She said it's a great place to go when you don't want to be surrounded by lots of people. Plus, the food is apparently simple but excellent.'

'You're spoiling me.'

'I'm glad to.' He opened the door to his car for her.

She slid in, pinching herself. When was the last time a man had taken such care of her getting into a car? Never, was the blunt answer. It might be an old-fashioned thing to do, but it gave her a sense of worth, as if she deserved to be treated well. He might also be being polite rather than relaxed and happy with her.

Danny got in but, instead of starting the engine, he turned to look at her. 'How have you been?'

'Great. I did quite a lot of cleaning-up outside, though the lawns still look a mess. It'll be a while before everything dries out and then there'll be dust for weeks, but the trees are all gone.' She'd put a fair bit of effort into hauling some of the branches away and her muscles had known about it for a couple of days.

'I kept wanting to walk out of the ED and come down to give you a hand. It would have been more fun than dealing with broken legs and heart attacks.' At last, a smile that went straight to *her* heart.

Where she shouldn't be letting it in. Not until she understood what had been behind his cooler approach when she'd opened her door. 'As a trainee doctor you're not meant to say things like that,' she retorted. 'How's your knee? You don't seem to be limping.' They hadn't talked all week. She'd tried phoning, but the connection in the Sounds was still intermittent, and unclear when it was working. Had Danny tried calling her?

'It's fine unless I make an impulsive turn or step too hard. Right, let's do this. We can talk over food and wine.'

And get the evening underway. She got it. 'Is the Nelson department busier than Blenheim's?'

'Lots more patients, but there are more staff to cover the cases most of the time. Though it was already heating up into the usual Friday night chaos when I left. One ED is the same as any other.' His voice had lifted and was filled with happiness.

'You like the work, don't you?'

He nodded.

'So why not specialise in emergency medicine? It's far more exciting than sitting at a computer reading X-rays, surely? You deal with people, not pictures.'

His smile slipped, and his hands tightened on the steering wheel for a moment. Concentrating on his driving a little too much, he didn't answer for a few minutes.

Here we go again.

Like those other times when she'd tried

to delve a little deeper into what drove him. Maybe she should tell him to pull over so she could get out and walk home.

Then he said, 'You're right, but I like the idea of studying those images and making decisions based on what's in front of me.'

No mention of patients. Was that a problem? Was there a reason involving a patient in the past behind why he wanted to be a radiologist? It didn't add up.

'You were good with the two people I delivered to ED earlier.'

'We all were. But there's something about radiology that fascinates me too.'

'I think I'd go raving mad not talking to people about what I was looking at. It's one of the reasons I left the lab.'

Danny's smile slowly returned.

Brooke worked on breathing easier. They were on their first date. She'd enjoy it, no matter what. Danny might relax a bit and talk about himself some more.

'I have hours on my own with no one to talk to, so to go to work and carry on the same would send me insane in a very short time.'

'Why don't you get a flatmate?'

'I didn't say I don't like being on my own. I just don't want to be that way twenty-four seven.' Leaning back in the seat, she watched the traffic going past in the opposite direction. 'I'd never lived by myself until I separated, and I enjoy it. Most of the time. There are days when I find myself talking to the birds, but usually it's great.'

'No arguments with yourself?'

'They're the best kind. I always win. And lose.'

'Here we go.' Danny parked opposite the restaurant and got out to open her door.

She could get used to this. It wasn't the most important characteristic in his make-up, but being a gentleman was always a bonus. 'Thank you.'

Taking her elbow, Danny walked them across the road and inside, where they were greeted by a young man dressed in black trousers and white shirt, who took their jackets before leading them to the furthest corner, where the windows looked out over the harbour.

'Look at that,' Brooke said with her heart in her throat. A ship was being nudged through the Cut by a tug with another one at the front with a wire strop running from the bow of the ship.

'Pretty awesome, isn't it?' Danny held her chair out, taking the job away from their waiter.

'Is the ship the reason for the slight shaking of the building?' Brooke asked the young man.

'Yes. Some people say it feels a bit like an earthquake.'

Exactly what she was thinking. Relief was instant.

'You've been in a few earthquakes?' Danny asked as he sat down opposite, his back to the rest of the restaurant.

'You're in New Zealand now, Danny. They're a regular occurrence, though not often very big. Growing up in Wellington, I've had more than my share of them. It's a shaky city, as well as the windiest.'

'Melbourne had one not too long ago which did some damage in the city centre. It was a complete shock to the locals. I was working on the children's ward and hadn't a clue what was going on. When someone yelled out "Earthquake!" I didn't believe them at first. They're rare there. But when people began diving for doorframes I got the idea it was for real.'

She was watching the ship as it was turned towards the main wharf further along. 'Incredible how something so huge can be manoeuvred like a floating toy.'

'Until it needs to stop.' Danny picked up the wine list. 'What wine do you prefer?'

'Chardonnay.'

Taking the menu the waiter was offering her, she began reading through the courses on offer. It was a short menu but looked awesome. 'How am I going to choose? Each dish sounds delicious.' Eventually she decided on the blue moki and salsa verde.

'I'm having the steamed mussels. We can share. Here's to us.' Danny tapped his glass of wine against hers. 'I am so happy to see you again.'

Here's to us.

That sounded as if he meant to continue their relationship a little longer at least. He was relaxing more and more.

She tapped back. 'To us.'

'Tell me more about what you do when you're not in the ambulance.'

'Apart from the upkeep on my house and going for runs, I like to spend time with my friends. Fairly ordinary, but I'm happy.' She wasn't about to mention she had begun writing a crime story. It was a work in progress with a long way to go.

'That's the main thing, isn't it?' He was watching her with something like envy.

'You're not happy doing what you do?' Would he answer, or once again dodge the question?

'I love my work.' So the problem was in his private life.

'What do you do for rest and relaxation?'

'Not a lot of time for those while I'm studying.' His gaze shifted to the night view outside.

Dodging was how it was going to be. Why? This was beginning to annoy her. If he had secrets then fine, but weren't they supposed to be getting to know each other?

'Fair enough,' she said a little too abruptly. 'Danny, I like you a lot, but you do seem to keep things close to your chest.' Not a bad chest either, but right now she wanted him to open up a little.

He came back to looking at her. 'You're right. I do.' He paused, seemed to be studying her and making up his mind about something.

She waited, the tip of her left boot tapping the carpet softly.

'It's a defence mechanism I've developed over the years. One day I'll explain why, but not tonight?'

She could see he was holding his breath. This must be important to him. Unfortunately for her, she understood how important it was to be allowed to have freedom to do and say whatever when it suited.

'All right.' Would she come to regret giving in to him so quickly? She *had* given in to him. Like she always had with her exes. Gave in. But Danny had asked for her patience. That was different. Or was she making excuses for herself? For him?

Looking away, she saw the lights of a small boat heading in through the Cut.

'I've let you down,' Danny said quietly.

She might have let herself down. Turning back to him, she saw the man she'd spent last weekend with, the kindness, the strength, his readiness to accept her as she was, and she sighed. She was taking a chance on Danny. She might be being gullible accepting his reticence to be open with her so far, but she'd give him the space he'd asked for, and wait until he was ready to talk—as long as he didn't take too long.

'No, you haven't. I'm fine with what you've said.'

His eyes widened in a startled expression, and now he reached for her hand. 'Thank you.'

Her heart expanded at the genuineness in those two words and his touch. With her free hand, she raised her glass. 'Let's enjoy our night out.'

'Let's.' The tension in Danny suddenly fell away and he gave her the devastating smile she'd been longing for all week. 'Here's to more of these.'

Yes, please. No matter what his problem,

she wanted to spend more time with Danny Collins.

'Are you ready to order?' The waiter was back.

The food was delicious, and the company just as delicious. She put everything behind her and enjoyed Danny. 'Do you want to come back to my place?' she asked as they walked hand in hand out to his car.

'Yes, please.' He kissed her. 'This is a great evening, Brooke.' And he kissed her again.

'I'm going to the market this morning,' Brooke told Danny as they stretched out in her bed after more sex. 'Want to come?'

And be surrounded by hundreds of people, any one of whom might recognise him? 'I don't do markets. I'll head back to the apartment and get some chores out of the way. Maybe catch up later? Go for a walk somewhere?'

'You don't know what you're missing out on. The Nelson market is one of the best. Everyone goes.'

Exactly. 'You're not going to change my mind.' He wrapped an arm around her waist and hugged in an effort to shift her off the subject.

Under his arm he felt her breathe deep and

huff it out. 'So it would seem.' She sounded peeved.

'You don't understand.'

'You're darned right I don't.' She pulled away, rolled out of bed.

He was still getting his head around the fact that Brooke hadn't learnt who Daniel Collins was. He'd been ultra-wary last night, unable to relax for a while. She obviously hadn't rushed to look him up on the internet. Not everyone did that, but he was so used to it happening to him he was struggling to accept Brooke hadn't. If she had and accepted him for himself, she'd still have said something or shown some reaction.

She knew his name, but nothing had really changed. He wanted to be with Brooke. He was close to loving her, if not already in love. It had happened fast. Possibly because for two days he wasn't looking over his shoulder for someone to shout out, 'Hey, Daniel Collins, what are you up to these days?'

Brooke was coming to mean so much to him, so that meant the time was fast approaching when he'd have to explain. But it was getting harder to face, not easier, because he had more to lose. He'd have to risk her changing to one of those women who'd let him down in the past. Granted Brooke was worth the risk.

He knew that. So why not get it over with? The sooner he found out how she'd react the sooner he could really let go the ties around his heart and be happy. Or the sooner he could tighten the knots and move on—again. He so wanted to know because he wanted to believe she would be different, because he longed for that future he'd dreamed of for years, and he wanted it with Brooke. It was early days as far as their relationship was concerned, but deep down he knew she meant so much more to him than he could've believed possible.

So do it. Tell her. Get it over with. Find out where he was headed. Suddenly it didn't seem too hard. He relaxed some and felt good. This would work out.

'Brooke...'

'I'm making the coffee and having a shower. I like to get to the market early, while the stalls are still full.' She headed out of the door, taking his chance to be open with her.

'Hang on. What's the hurry?'

Give me a minute. More like half an hour.

Glancing over her bare shoulder, she shrugged at him. 'Whatever you were about to say will have to wait. The best fruit and vegetable stalls sell out fast.'

He swore under his breath as he watched her walk away. Women didn't walk off from him.

They swooned and made all sorts of ridiculous promises. This was new, and he liked it, but his head thumped with despair. What if he never got it right with Brooke? He'd finally decided to do the right thing and the opportunity walked out of the door. He could've called her back, but it didn't feel right. Brooke was on a mission, and not happy with him. To stop her to talk about himself might not start off well.

Not using that as an excuse, by any chance?

He didn't think so.

'I'll make the coffee while you're in the shower,' he called after her, shivering as he tossed the covers aside. This was one cold house. Being a nineteen-twenties building, there probably wasn't any insulation in the walls or roof. What would it cost to fix? Was it even possible? The inner walls would have to be pulled apart at some place to be able to spray the insulation behind them. A costly job which might be beyond her. Plus the rooms he'd seen appeared to have had a lot of decorating done, which no doubt Brooke wouldn't want ruined. He might be able to talk to her about it later, if they were still getting along. They had to be. There was no other way forward.

Showered and dressed in last night's clothes, Danny stood at the bench gulping coffee and toast. Brooke's foot was tapping the floor and she kept glancing at the oven clock.

'It's meant to rain later. We might have to postpone the walk. Do you do movies? As in go to a theatre?' She was watching him carefully. Waiting for him to say he didn't do movies either?

'A bit old-fashioned, isn't it?' Even if the place was full they'd be in the dark, so no one would notice him. 'But, yeah, why not? What's on?'

Brooke passed over her phone and he read the list of films showing locally. 'Not a lot of choice unless you like dancing piglets.'

For the first time that morning she laughed.

And the tension in his gut backed off some. He wasn't out of trouble by a long shot, but he had a bit more time on hand. Brooke really did have him wound around her little finger.

'I'll settle for the crime wave if that suits you.' He'd seen the pile of books beside her bed, all thrillers. Something else they had in common. The list grew every day. The time to be upfront with her was rushing at him.

Do it. Get it out of the way for ever so you can relax completely.

'Perfect.' She gathered up some shopping bags. 'Not rushing you but I'm heading out in a few minutes.'

'Yes, you are,' he told her, relieved there wasn't time to talk now. She was in a hurry, and he was backing away from opening up to her. This had to stop. 'Brooke?'

'Yes?' Her foot was tapping the door mat impatiently.

This was clearly not a good time to hold her up. So, 'Which time slot do you want to go to the movie?' He'd probably come up with that excuse to save his heart. Too late now. He'd have to wait it out for another appropriate moment.

'How about five? Then we could grab a meal at the pub afterwards.' She was heading for the door, not realising he wanted her to stay so he could talk to her.

'Or we could get takeaways and go back to the apartment.'

She blinked in surprise, looking a bit like a dingo caught in headlights. Except no dingoes in NZ. 'We could?'

'Why not?' Because he had been closed off so far. He understood her surprise and felt ashamed. 'I'd like to show you where I'm living while I'm here.' He'd go to the supermarket this morning to get some steak and other bits and pieces to cook for dinner and show her he was more than a doctor of no long-term abode.

He'd let her in a bit more by sharing what he had here. 'The views are stunning.'

It would be pitch dark beyond the harbour, but the Western Ranges would become visible when the sun rose in the morning. To see the mountains beyond Tasman Bay was magic, unlike anything he'd opened his curtains to in Australia. It didn't matter how chilly the mornings had been in the past week, he'd taken his first coffee of the day on the deck, absorbing the sight.

At last Brooke relaxed fully. 'Meet you at the theatre? I'll walk. You know where it is?'

'I have a phone. Sure you don't want me to pick you up?' Every minute spent with Brooke was another enjoyed—until she learned the truth.

'It's only five minutes from here.'

There was no arguing with that tone. It dawned on him Brooke wanted time to herself. She had said she was happy with her own company, and here he was wanting every minute with her he could get. Was it because she wasn't as keen on him as he was her? Or had she become ultra-cautious after her failed relationship? He couldn't see that, considering how quickly they'd first got together sexually, and how he'd stayed in her place for the rest of his short time in the bay. So she was used to being alone and having him here in her space was fine until she was ready for a break.

'Not a problem.' She wouldn't know what he was really referring to. 'I'll see you there.'

'That wasn't the most enthralling script,' Brooke said, slipping her arm through Danny's as they walked to his car. 'I worked out who the antagonist was about halfway through.' All the notes on writing crime came with one firm instruction—be sure not to give away too many clues too early.

'I wasn't far behind you. It was disappointing considering the fantastic cast.'

He was right. They were all big names in the film industry. 'Still better than the dancing piglets.' A cold, wet gust of wind hit them, and she snuggled closer to Danny. He felt so good, like the man of her dreams. She could get used to always having him at her side. If he wasn't only a dream. Her elbow nudged into his side. No, he was real. Sexy real. Fun real. Interesting real. Make that not entirely real yet, because there were things he hesitated to talk about.

But had she told him all her problems? she wondered. Her problems weren't so bad she couldn't talk about them. She wasn't mentioning them to Danny yet because it was too early in their relationship, which might be his answer to her concerns. Too early to be delving into the deep stuff. So when did they? His hesitancy made her cautious, and worried she'd be sorry for giving him space. It would be too late if they waited until they'd fallen in love, and it hurt more if the other person wasn't happy about what they learned.

Only one way to find out. If she wanted to, and she could say for certain she did. She was falling for this gorgeous man, fast and deep. Even when she sensed there was a lot to learn about him, like that morning when he didn't want to go to the market with her. It was only a market, not a major event. But, despite her caution, he was getting to her in ways she hadn't known before. He was different to other men she'd been serious about in that he put her first, or at least was at her side. He'd been quick to help with Lloyd, while not acting as though he'd done all the work, had credited her with saving Lloyd with her insistence on going into that house. Not once had he put her down or questioned her take on something. She couldn't stop feeling Danny would never do that. This wasn't a charade to be dropped once she'd been sucked in. He read her well, hopefully not so well that she couldn't keep some things to herself for a while.

'Where have you gone again?' Danny asked as they climbed into his car. 'Not going over what happened in the movie, I hope.'

'Wondering what you're cooking for my dinner.' See? He did get her. He'd caught her out mind-wandering and hadn't demanded to know what she was thinking about or what had he done to upset her. He wasn't putting himself first. That was special in her book.

'Wait and see,' he said with a laugh. 'But don't get too excited. I'm not a gourmet chef.'

'Steak then. Or fish.'

Another deep belly laugh filled the car. 'I knew you'd get it. I can promise you it's not kangaroo. There don't seem to be any in this country. Plenty of wild wallabies though, I'm told.'

'They're taking over some of the bush country. You might be able to find some in the ranges. Might keep you from getting homesick.'

'*If* I was ever homesick it wouldn't be because I hadn't seen a kangaroo in a while.'

He was still laughing happily, tempting Brooke to ask what might cause that emotion, but she didn't want to bring on that stillness some of her questions invoked. Old Brooke to the fore? Protecting herself from being lied to or conned into doing something she didn't want? She didn't believe so. That Brooke was gone. This Brooke wanted to enjoy being with Danny and still be true to herself. She didn't need to dig into who he was. She could wait to be drip fed bits and pieces as they spent more time together.

'Have you eaten kangaroo steak? I hear it's to die for.'

'Delizioso.' He smacked his lips together. 'This is making the steak seem ordinary.'

'No way. I love steak but hardly ever cook it.' They were passing a supermarket. 'Can you stop? I'll get a bottle of Pinot Noir.'

'All sorted.'

'Damn, but I could get to like you.' Too late. She already did, and like had already turned into something closer to love.

'So my plan's working.'

The rest of his plan appeared straightforward. They shared dinner, coffee and bed. And in the morning they made slow, idyllic love and ate breakfast wrapped in blankets sitting on the tiny deck overlooking the harbour and out to Tasman Bay. The day flew by. Brooke enjoyed doing nothing, lazing around talking, being quiet, laughing, making love again, eating. Perfect, really.

After a light snack on Sunday night, she finally pulled on her boots and headed for the door, Danny behind her. Turning around, she wound her arms around him and held on tight. 'Thank you for a great weekend.'

He kissed her forehead. 'Back at you.'

'I'm on nights this week.' At work, that was, not getting close and sexy in her bed.

'I've got a mix of afternoons and mornings. We'll probably cross paths in ED some time.'

He could've sounded a little disappointed that they wouldn't have time together.

'I'll wish for an accident where no one gets hurt but needs to be taken to ED anyway.'

'You'd never do that.'

No, but it had been worth saying just to see that ridiculously sexy smile. If only she didn't feel so happy with him, didn't feel a growing apprehension that there was a bomb waiting to explode.

CHAPTER EIGHT

'Hey, sis, how's things?'

'Apart from missing out on our week together, I'm good,' Saskia replied. 'Though the bank account took a hit last week. I mean, what's a girl supposed to do when her holiday plans are changed?'

Laughing, Brooke retorted, 'Hit the shops and buy an outrageous number of clothes.' She got it. 'New suits to wear to court, matching high end shoes and handbags.' Saskia was a lawyer and liked to look the part. 'I should've come over to join you instead of staying on at the bach.' It would've been hard to walk away from the mess that had become the yard, though. She hadn't wanted her parents to have to go there to do the job.

'I did say that.'

'I know.' They'd talked a few times over the week. Brooke hadn't mentioned Danny other than to say he'd helped her with Lloyd and some cleaning up. 'Like I need more clothes.' Her wardrobe was chock full of lovely clothes from previous shopping expeditions with Saskia, and she wore a uniform to work.

'You sound tired. What's up?'

She could never hide anything from her sister. 'Had a busy weekend, that's all.' She had spent a lot of time worrying about what was going on with Danny and herself. Even more time having fun, and not a lot of sleep last night as they'd got together in his oh, so comfy bed.

'You weren't working, so what kept you busy?'

This was really why she'd rung. She wanted to talk to Saskia about Danny, but still she hesitated.

'Come on. Spill. Is it something to do with that doctor staying at Paula and Mike's?'

'How do you do that?'

'I know you. So it was. Danny, wasn't it?'

'Yeah.' She sighed. 'I… We got close, very close.'

'He must be special then.'

Brooke agreed. *He is.* 'We'd been rescuing Lloyd from his falling down house, and me falling and being swept towards the beach, and, I don't know, just having a few frights. Afterwards we kind of came together and let rip.'

'Have you seen him since he left the bay?'

'We spent the weekend together. He's working in Nelson ED.'

'What aren't you telling me, Brooke?'

She sighed. She shouldn't have rung Saskia, but her sister was her best friend. 'I really, really like him, as in I might be falling for him.'

'You're afraid he'll hurt you.'

Got it in one. 'I get the sense that he's holding back on me. Am I being too cautious? It is early days, and I'm probably expecting too much.'

'You could try looking him up on the internet,' Saskia said, then laughed. 'You won't though. You want him to talk to you straight up.'

'I do. If we're going to have a relationship then it should be open and honest.'

'Then you're going to have to be patient. Not one of your strongest traits these days,' Saskia said. 'It is only a few days since you met though, and in that time you were stranded together in the midst of chaos, then returned separately to Nelson and your jobs. Give him a chance, Brooke. Someone might've hurt him in the past too, making him as wary as you.'

'Thanks, Sash. I had considered that, but needed to hear it from someone else. It's just that he is gorgeous and I can feel myself falling under his spell.'

'Then get out there and make the most of him, leave the worries alone for a bit. You are stronger these days, you can fight for yourself.'

Brooke put her phone down with a sense of relief. Nothing had changed, or been solved, but she was ready to continue with Danny as things were for a while longer. Hopefully he felt the same. And if he didn't, then so be it.

Really?

No, but she was trying to be positive about the future.

Danny watched the young woman on the bed. She was calming down as the anaphylaxis stopped, the panic slowly fading from her face. The epinephrine he'd administered within minutes of her being brought into the department had prevented serious constriction to her breathing.

Relief poured through him. With anaphylactic shocks there was always that moment when he didn't know which way the outcome would go. The paramedic's urgency and one fast check of Jamie and he'd been drawing up the drug to save her. Turning to the man standing in the corner of the cubicle looking frightened by what had happened, Danny said, 'You did the right thing calling the ambulance as soon as you did and bringing that bottle of pills was even better. It gave us a heads-up to what was causing Jamie's distress.'

'You think the penicillin did this?'

'Yes.'

'She only had one tablet. It wasn't like she'd taken too many.' The guy didn't relax.

'Sometimes the drug will build up in a person's system until the body can't take it any more and then they'll have a reaction. Unfortunately, a small percentage of people have an instant shock and that's often severe.'

'What happens now?'

'I'm keeping Jamie here so she can be monitored for a while, and we can make sure she's going to be all right. Then she'll go to a general ward and be administered a new antibiotic for the infection in her surgical wound.' Jamie had had her appendix removed the previous week.

'I can't thank you enough, Doc. I'm going to be paranoid about any pills she takes from now on.'

'You can relax. Her doctors will be aware of what's happened and they'll make sure she's safe. Pull up a chair and sit with her. I'll be back later.'

Danny checked the case list, found no one needing him and went to grab a much-needed coffee at the cafeteria. An hour to go before knock-off time, which meant nothing, as none of the staff left just because the clock had ticked over to shift-finish hour.

'How's it going?' The cardiologist he'd called in earlier for a patient with heart oedema was sitting at a table near where he was waiting for his coffee.

'I've had better days.'

'Haven't we all? What do you do for relaxation?'

'As little as possible. Go for runs mostly.' Spend time with Brooke now she was back in town.

'You don't play golf?'

Alarm bells rang, but when Danny looked directly at the guy he wasn't staring at him as if it was a loaded question.

'Not at all. I'm useless at it.'

'I'm sorry to hear that.'

Jackson knew. Danny could swear he did.

'Can't be helped.'

'If you ever want to hit a ball around on a Sunday morning give me a bell. I'm not great, but I like getting out and stretching the body a bit.' Jackson drained his coffee and stood up. 'No pressure. Just thought you might want to meet some of the crew away from here.'

'Thanks.' If he was going to be comfortable

living here then this was what he should do. The day would come when he'd have to get over himself.

'Greg from Radiology plays too. You've met him? He's a good bloke.' That was a recommendation? Probably as good as they got from this man.

Danny couldn't help himself. He said, 'I don't have any clubs. Not with me anyway. I presume the club hires them out.' What was he doing even considering this?

'They do.' Jackson handed him a card. 'My numbers if you decide to join us.'

'Again, thanks.'

'No problem. By the way, you did a good job with Mrs Hogarth. She's got a good chance of a full recovery, thanks to your fast action.'

Danny shook his head at him. 'Not me. It's the paramedic, who saved her first time round when she was at her worst.' Not Brooke this time, but another competent medic. Would he see Brooke before he left for the day? He hoped so.

Jackson smiled. 'You should definitely make an effort to join us for a game. See you around.'

The guy headed away, leaving Danny feeling as though he'd just made a friend without even trying. Nelson was turning out to be good for him.

* * *

'Morning.' Danny was leaning against the wall at the central ambulance station when Brooke walked outside the next morning at the end of her shift.

'Howdy. What are you doing here at this hour?'

'Waiting to take you to breakfast before you hit the sack. And I don't mean I'm joining you in said sack. You've worked a twelve-hour night shift. I'm sure you're exhausted.' There was a twinkle in his eye that said he might be available if she wasn't shattered.

'What other plans have you got for the morning?' she asked, stalling on her answer just to tease him. She was tired, but not so much that a good romp in bed was off the list.

'Study.'

'What about getting out and about?'

'On a Tuesday morning when everyone I know is working? Not that I've had time to get to know people very well, other than you.' His eyes widened a little, then returned to normal. Had he just lied?

That unease was back. That romp not quite so enticing. Not make love with Danny? Impossible to turn down. This was getting silly.

'Since you said you play golf occasionally,

why not have a game at the club and meet people there?'

'I might just do that,' he said indifferently. 'One of the surgeons suggested it the other day.'

Danny had answered her, no hesitation at all. That threw her. She was used to him avoiding questions. She could relax a bit for now.

'Where shall we go for breakfast?' No more questions about golf or friends or he might clam up again.

'I was hoping you'd know somewhere good. I feel like a full works brekkie.'

'Let's go.'

'Thought you were never going to say yes.' He led her to his car.

Maybe I shouldn't have.

'I've been asked to cover for someone on Sunday.'

'The reality of being a paramedic, eh?' Danny said. 'No matter, I've got plenty to be doing. I've been ignoring study over the past few days. A certain lady keeps distracting me.'

'Don't go blaming me if you fail your exams,' she warned. 'I take no responsibility at all.'

'Now there's a surprise. You're not geared to spend your time trying to please me, are you?' he said with his best sexy grin.

Little did he realise how close he was to

knowing who she used to be. 'Never,' she replied a little too sharply.

His grin dipped. 'Did I hit a nerve?'

There was nothing to lose by explaining and it might encourage Danny to be more open with her. 'I'm not a pleaser.' Not any more. 'Not to the point where I give up everything I want anyway.'

'Go on.'

She had his full attention now, almost as though he wasn't used to people talking about themselves in more than a casual way. 'One day my ex picked me up from work and said we were moving to a new flat at the end of the week. I hadn't even known he was looking to change homes.'

'Hardly fair or thoughtful.'

'Another time he nearly bankrupted us by buying a property before we'd sold the house we already owned. We couldn't afford that.'

'You weren't consulted about that move either?'

'No.'

'No wonder he's your ex.'

'I didn't walk away easily. We were a couple. Don't couples support each other? There was the rub. He was never going to change. I was the one who was supposed to get over it, move on, be happy. Great when I didn't know when

I got home every night what shock might be awaiting me. I was the one who'd have to sort out the financial losses and work extra hours to pay the bills. I left him.'

'How'd he take that?'

Danny got it in one 'He hated it. Me. I was supposed to love him and understand he was trying to do great things for us.' *Yeah, right.* 'If only I'd seen him for what he was a lot earlier.'

'But you did eventually, and that's what counts.' An arm went around her shoulders and he drew her in close. 'You're tougher than you realise.'

'Most of the time. I know I won't let anyone control me like that again.'

'No one should want to. Nor do they have the right.' Danny kissed her forehead.

'It's made me very wary of people keeping secrets. I always wonder what their agenda is. Am I being duped again?'

The arm around her shoulders tensed. Danny drew a long, slow breath. Then he said quietly, 'Stay strong. You'll be okay.'

'What are you not saying, Danny?'

'That I think you're amazing. Everything I've seen about you, from that storm to bringing patients into ED to spending time with me, you're strong, considerate and kind. Your ex was a fool.'

Brooke relaxed. He'd tensed because she'd been hurt, no other reason. She'd been letting her suspicious mind take over the logical side. Or had she excused him because she didn't want to go there?

'Do you want to come home with me for an hour or so?' They could talk over another coffee, clear the air a bit.

'Now let me think.' Danny looked around with a smile crossing his mouth. Then he turned and grabbed her to him and began kissing her like there was no tomorrow.

Brooke wanted to pull back and have it out with him, but his kiss was burning her up, turning all sensible thought to chaos. She gave in and went with him. There wouldn't be a lot of talking involved right now.

So Brooke had walked away from her ex because he was unstable when it came to being settled. It sounded to Danny that financially they'd been doing all right until Brad got carried away and nearly bankrupted them.

After returning to his apartment to let Brooke get some much-needed sleep, Danny sat on his deck, looking out over Tasman Bay, the view not quite as beguiling today. Hearing Brooke's story, however brief, gave him more insight into who she was and why she was wary of him when he didn't always answer her questions about himself. She'd had a few hard knocks along the way, but she seemed to have done fine by herself. She had that house right in town and was doing it up. She was a top-notch paramedic and was happy with her life.

What did she want for her future? A partner to have a home and family with was probably part of her dreams. Did she want a grander lifestyle? To be financially secure? Not be the only one paying the mortgage on that house? Houses in Nelson didn't come cheap. He'd looked them up the other day for interest's sake. Or in case he got close with Brooke and decided to make this town his home. But now the old doubts were tumbling back into his head. Would she see his wealth as something to grab hold of, so she didn't have to fear losing everything? Brad hadn't kept her up-to-date with his plans. *He* hadn't told her his past. Was she going to see *him* in the same light as her ex?

It did explain some things. But he was none the wiser about how she'd react to his past. He very much doubted Brooke would turn out to be like the other women in his life and see him as a ticket out of her life—which she said she was happy with—to something bigger and more secure.

He had no issues with making her feel secure, he even wanted that. He especially needed to make her feel loved for herself. The feelings he had for Brooke were special, and overwhelming, and loving. He loved her. But was he ready to lay his heart on the line and wait to see what she did with it?

The clock was ticking, and he would be outed if he delayed any longer. Brooke hearing his story from him was better than someone else telling her. It was a matter of trust, which he'd deliberately been overlooking in a bid to protect himself. It was going to backfire if he didn't pull his finger out and get on with it.

His phone interrupted his gloomy thoughts.

'Hey, Danny, it's Jackson. I know I said to give me a call if you wanted a game, but Troy and I were booked to play this afternoon and he can't make it. I see you're working the night shift. Want to take his place?'

He didn't hesitate. Brooke was getting much-needed sleep before her next shift, and he needed a distraction.

'Count me in. What time and where?'

As he listened to the details, Danny couldn't believe he'd accepted Jackson's offer so readily. It would be a badly needed distraction and might go some way to quieting the turmoil in his head. He did love Brooke, and the deeper in he got, the more concerned he was about to have his heart slammed.

But there was a conversation he needed to have with her. The sooner the better. Not today though. He had a game of golf to play.

'Marie Coupland, forty-one, fell down flight of stairs in her home, suspected fractured right arm, shoulder damage, lacerations to head and legs.' Brooke handed the paperwork to the ED nurse indicating which cubicle to take the patient.

'Any obvious head injuries?' Danny came up behind her.

'There don't appear to be. Conscious level's good,' Brooke answered, trying not to smile too wide as everyone lifted the woman onto the bed from the stretcher. This was the first time she'd seen Danny since Tuesday morning in bed. Their rosters hadn't matched and besides he was supposed to be studying. It wasn't for her to keep him away from that. But now it was Friday, she was coming towards the end of her shift, and she had tomorrow free. So did Danny, if she'd read the roster correctly.

'Marie, I'm Danny, the doctor who'll be attending you. Did you at any time lose consciousness? Maybe before the ambulance crew reached you?'

'I don't think so. I had to crawl a few metres to get my phone to call 111. I felt a lot of pain but I was aware of what I was doing all the time.'

'We had to untangle her legs when we got there,' Corina, the ambulance officer on with Brooke, told Danny. Her eyes lit up with excitement as she locked them on him.

Brooke was not amused. They were here for a patient, not to flirt with the staff. Was that a twinge of jealousy? Glancing at Danny, she relaxed. He was focused entirely on Marie, carefully touching her scalp, searching for any tender spots. She hadn't found any, but it was his job to make certain. Then she noticed his mouth had flattened. Because he had found an injury? Or because Corina had annoyed him?

The pager on her belt beeped. Time to go. Another callout needed an urgent response. Reaching for the stretcher, Brooke started for the ambulance bay. 'Come on, Corina. We've got a Code Three down at the port.'

'Coming. See you later, Doctor.'

Danny didn't respond.

Brooke smiled to herself. She might tease him about this when they next got together. Hopefully that night when he finished at eleven, except he rarely walked off the job immediately. There was nearly always a patient he was midway through helping, or an influx of urgent patients just as shift change was occurring.

'What've we got?' Corina asked as she strapped herself in and began driving out of the bay.

'A crane driver loading logs has fallen off his machine and is unconscious.' Brooke put the siren and lights on to alert the traffic. 'Our patient's going to have more than a head injury. Those cranes are so tall it's creepy.'

'That's what I'm thinking too.' Corina's disposition was calm as she weaved through cars moving out of the way. Same as when she dealt with severely injured patients. She'd make a good paramedic by the time she'd finished her training. It was how she'd behaved around Danny that annoyed Brooke and, to be fair, she wasn't sure if that was her being antsy because he was her man.

Swallowing her annoyance, she said, 'It's been a night for falls.' First Marie, and now this case.

Mark Dixon wasn't going to be driving a crane for a long time to come. 'Severe head injuries, fractured upper arm and shoulder, query spinal damage as there was no reaction to pressure on his feet. He was lying at an odd angle when we got there.' Brooke filled Danny and another doctor in when they brought him back to the ED. 'Fortunately no one tried to move him. His heart rate dipped, then stopped on the way in and I had to get Corina to pull over so we could resuscitate him.'

Mark was transferred from the spinal board to a bed in Resus. Brooke read through the notes she'd written up so far, added more while watching Danny and the female doctor begin assessing what lay before them. Where did they begin with a case like this? Damage to the spine needed urgent attention, but the head injuries were worse, and if there was internal bleeding, as she suspected, that would need fast intervention. Who'd be a doctor?

'Here you go.' She handed the paperwork to a nurse.

Danny took the pages from the nurse, gave it a quick glance. 'That's one heck of a fall.'

'Yes. Right onto concrete.' She gave him a small private smile. 'We'll leave you to it.'

'See you, Dr Danny,' Corina called over her shoulder as she took the stretcher away.

Again, Danny's mouth flattened, and he turned back to his patient without a word. Corina was undoubtedly annoying him.

'You do know who he is, don't you?' Corina

asked the moment Brooke got into the ambulance, this time as the driver.

'Who?' But she knew who Corina was referring to. Dr Danny.

'Danny…aka Daniel Collins. I'd swear that's him. He's got the looks and the body, and his smile is to die for.'

'So?' Now she thought about it, his surname wasn't on his badge. Most doctors at the hospital had their full name on their badge, but Danny wore one that wasn't hospital issue, reading Dr Danny. Why not Daniel Collins if that was who he really was? Was he hiding something? Like who he was?

'So Daniel Collins is famous.'

'For what?' The steering wheel was tight in her palms, and her foot hit the brake too hard as she slowed before driving out onto the main road. Had she been burying her head when it came to Danny not talking about himself? But everyone had the right to remain silent unless it affected someone else, and she couldn't see how anything about Danny being famous could affect her so there wasn't an issue.

Except he didn't tell me. Not even a hint.

She had given him some leeway, hoping she'd hear more soon. Had she been too trusting? Or too far in love to look beyond the surface? Not again. Anything but that. No, this wasn't her doing. Danny had held back, not her. He hadn't trusted her with the truth. He'd been happy to listen to her past problems and keep his own to himself. He'd betrayed her trust. Betrayed her love. It was beyond hurtful. He knew how she'd been hurt and yet he hadn't said a word. Not one. Well, Daniel Collins, you're done for.

Corina was looking at her phone. 'Daniel Collins, Australian, thirty-two, three times junior world golf champion, winner of US junior competitions, Australian, Asian, New Zealand, British competitions. Want me to go on?'

'Not really.' Not at all. She didn't want Corina reading out anything to do with Danny. Sorry, Daniel Collins. She'd look him up herself when she got home, and the door was locked and she'd had a shower. Why had he stopped playing? The next step would surely have been into the open league.

'Base to Nelson Ambulance One.'

Thank goodness for radios and work. Brooke held her breath while Corina took the call. If this wasn't a case to attend, she'd go back to base and hide out in the bathroom until home time.

'Nelson Ambulance One receiving.'

'Possible breech birth, woman alone, says

she's bleeding.' The woman at base gave an address.

Corina acknowledged the call and began writing down the few details they were receiving.

Brooke turned on the lights. 'Here we go again. It's been a busy shift.'

Thank God it was nearly over. She kept talking to shut Corina down about Danny. Her head was whirling. Danny wasn't Danny. He was Daniel Collins, apparently a famous golf player. Big deal. It wasn't something she couldn't handle—other than that he'd never mentioned it. What else hadn't he mentioned?

Daniel Collins…born and raised in a comfortable lifestyle in Ballarat, Victoria. He had a brother who was a CEO of some technology company in Canada, and his father owned an investment company that was rated very highly.

Daniel Collins had done exceptionally well in his golfing career, winning all those competitions Corina had read out and plenty more. He'd earned millions after he turned nineteen and became a professional player.

Daniel Collins's career had plummeted at age twenty-one when he dived into a pool to rescue a drowning four-year-old boy at a millionaire's home in Los Angeles. He'd damaged his shoulder and ribs and could no longer swing a golf club as well as he had in the past. But he'd become an overnight hero for saving the film producer's son. He had wanted to make a movie featuring Daniel. Daniel had talked him out of it.

There were many photos of Daniel Collins with glamorous women hanging off his immaculate suit-covered arm. Brooke swallowed the urge to throw up.

Daniel Collins was now studying to become a doctor in Melbourne.

That was slightly out-of-date.

Brooke pushed her laptop away and picked up the mug of tea she'd made after her shower.

Daniel Collins.

The name went round and round in her head.

Not Danny, but Daniel.

He had hidden who he was from her. Fair enough? Or plain, damned insulting? Was he hiding the truth from her in case she thought she could make the most of his wealth? Or want the limelight? Though when she thought about it he seemed to want to avoid that at all costs. This explained the restaurant table by the window where he sat with his back to the other diners and preferring to eat at home than go to the pub, and wearing that name badge at work.

Another gulp of tea. He had hidden who he was from *her*. Okay, she got that he mightn't want to spout off about his past, but not to tell her his name or where he'd grown up or the places he'd visited? No, she wasn't letting him off so easily. She'd been sucked in before, and now Danny had done the same. She'd thought he was a regular, good guy working hard to become a doctor. He *was* all of those, but there was so much more. What happened when the media confronted him? Did he play up to them, or go all quiet? Did he love or hate the limelight?

More tea went down her throat. Whatever. She didn't care. He'd been playing her along. And she was done with men who did that. Even her mother had had to learn not to keep things of importance from her. What Danny— he was still Danny to her despite what she'd learned—had done wasn't as bad by a long shot, but it was wrong as far as she was concerned. More than that, they were barely two weeks into their relationship. What would happen further down the track?

It was time to have a talk. He deserved the chance to explain.

Problem being he was at work and wouldn't

finish for another five hours. By then she'd be wound up like a clock, her springs ready to burst wide, opening up to let everything through without touching the wires that usually kept her together.

She texted him.

Please come here when you finish work.

Then she sat back, finished a second mug of tea, and waited. And waited.

He didn't answer. By eleven she was pacing the floor. Would he drop by? Would he go to his apartment for a sleep after a busy night? Well, he wasn't getting one. She snatched up her keys and headed out of the door.

Danny heard the buzzer. Someone wanted to see him. As far as he was aware, only Brooke knew where he lived. Had to be her. Had to be. But he'd replied to her text saying he'd catch up later when he'd had some shut-eye. He needed time to himself.

He'd been outed earlier by that ambulance officer. Corina had been waiting for him when he took his dinner break at the staff cafeteria. He'd known immediately by the way she'd smiled at him. It was all so familiar, so gut-wrenching. He didn't want this now, not when he and Brooke were getting on so well, when he'd begun to think he could have a normal life.

He loved Brooke. He'd held off telling her who he used to be for too long, and now he'd pay the price. It was all very well feeling relaxed and happy in a way he hadn't for so long—maybe since he'd first begun to make a name for himself in golf—but he'd known this day would arrive.

The buzzer sounded again, almost angry with him.

'Yes?'

'Can I come up?'

Brooke's voice was angry. Corina had probably filled her in on all the details.

'Of course.' His heart dropped. What was she going to say? Do?

He opened the door and waited. His heart was now pounding, and his legs didn't feel strong enough to hold him up for much longer. Everything rested on the next few minutes.

The elevator door slid open and there she was, looking fierce. 'Daniel.'

Bang. Daniel. She knew.

'Brooke.' He stepped back, his hand holding the door to the apartment wide. 'Come in.'

She strode past him, back straight, head high, and went through to the lounge, where she stopped by the glass doors looking over the bay. Her gaze was directed outside, but he knew her mind was right in the room, focused on him and how he'd let her down.

'I'm sorry,' Danny said with everything he had in him. He was so sorry it hurt.

Brooke spun around. 'Not good enough, Daniel.'

That made him mad. He wasn't Daniel to Brooke. He was Danny. Had always been Danny, the man who was at ease with her.

'Don't, Brooke. I've messed up, but don't make it worse.'

'Really? Finding out from someone else who you are doesn't make this worse? For me, it does. What's more, you know why I feel like that.'

'Let me explain.'

'You've had two weeks to explain, or at least give me an inkling. You could've told me when I talked about Brad and how he'd hidden important stuff from me.'

'I wanted to.'

'Then why didn't you?' she snarled. 'It's taken me finding out from another source for you to offer that.'

She wasn't making it easy, but who could blame her?

'I was wrong. But I was so happy with you and I didn't want it to stop.'

'You didn't—'

He held his hand up in a stop position.

'Brooke, believe me when I say I knew I was dicing with trouble, but I've never felt as relaxed with anyone as I have with you these past weeks. It's not what I'm used to, and I couldn't give it up.'

'You already made up your mind how I'd react? Good one, Danny. Thanks for the vote of confidence.'

Breathe in, slowly breathe out. This wasn't Brooke's fault. He shouldn't be angry with her. But there was so much to lose. If he hadn't already lost her. *Breathe in, slowly breathe out.*

'Please sit down. This could take a while.'

For a moment Brooke didn't move.

Breathe in, slowly breathe out.

She crossed to the couch and sat upright, her hands clasped in her lap. Not a Brooke pose he'd seen before. It suggested she was more than angry with him, she was hurt. He had to fight himself not to haul her into his arms and promise everything would be all right. That wasn't the way to go with Brooke. She'd never let him get away with that. She deserved his story before anything else.

Sitting on the arm of a lounge chair, he swallowed hard. 'I take it you've read about my career in golf?'

'It's all there at the tap of an icon, every last detail. You were quite something. Still are, from what I gathered.'

'Yes. It doesn't go away, even though I no longer have anything to do with the upper echelon golfing world. I'm being unrealistic to even wish it would, I know.' Had always known. 'I was young when I first caught attention from players, coaches, and the media. I tried not to let it go to my head, but I lost that battle. I enjoyed being in the limelight. Reporters wanted to know everything about me, and I mean everything, right down to the brand of socks I wore for a golf match. Some people love that. It drove me crazy at times but it was the price I had to pay for being famous.' Along with the women who liked to cling to his arm.

Brooke stared at him. 'I can believe that.'

So she wasn't going to knock him down over everything. Dared he relax? Her gaze remained steady and didn't show any of her usual friendliness.

So stay on guard, protect your heart, though it's probably too late for that.

'Then I was invited to a pool party at a friend's in LA and everything changed.' She'd

have read what had happened so no need to re-
count the details that had heightened his fame.
'My golfing career was over, and I struggled
for a while. I wasn't hopping on planes to fly
all over the world. I didn't have to get out of
bed to go to the range to practice a stroke. I
didn't have a purpose in life. It was strange,
and yet reporters were still following me,
asking what I was going to do next. Would
I become a coach? Would I do this…do that?
Blah-blah-blah.'

'Plus putting it out there that you were a hero
for saving that little boy.'

He sighed. 'Yeah. As if anyone wouldn't
have done what I did. I happened to see Toby
go under for the second time when no one else
did. He wasn't moving his limbs and I reacted.'

'You injured yourself and still pulled him
out, probably adding to your injuries.' Was that
admiration in her voice?

If it was, he didn't want it. She didn't owe
him a thing.

'True.'

The doctors told him he'd also tweaked his
spine lifting the boy off the bottom of the pool.

'So why couldn't you tell me this? It's part
of who you are.'

'There's an ugly side to all this.' *Breathe
in. Slowly breathe out.* 'I was in a relationship

when I had to give up golf. Iris loved being in front of the cameras and wasn't pleased she hadn't been there when I saved Toby. Like it was my fault for not taking her with me, but she wasn't in the US at the time. Whenever I was interviewed about that day she made sure she was there. Then she started going on about how I should start touring countries and get paid to talk about my career and encouraging others to do the same.'

Brooke remained quiet. He wasn't sure what that meant.

'Money was right up there with the glamour for Iris. The crunch came when I decided to apply for med school back in Melbourne. She was furious, said it wouldn't bring in the same money, and that I'd be stuck looking after people and unable to socialise with important people. I began to see I mightn't have loved her as much as I'd thought. I certainly didn't want to continue with the relationship the way it was, and she didn't want to go with my plans. We split up. To this day I think she probably sticks pins in a voodoo doll before she goes to bed every night.'

'No wonder you wince in your sleep sometimes.' Brooke's posture had softened a little.

Hope flared, until Danny knocked it back in place. He had hurt this wonderful woman by not sharing who he was. All he could hope for was that she'd understand what had driven him.

'That could be due to many reasons,' he replied.

'Why medicine?' He had once mentioned this briefly.

'Before golf became my career, I thought I'd study medicine. I was good at science subjects at school and fascinated with biology, and especially after the conversations my grandpa and I had when I was younger. When I finally got over what had happened it was a given really that I'd go to med school. I had to do a fair bit of study to get in, it having been a few years since I'd looked at a science book.'

'You're obviously happy with your decision. You're good at what you do.' Brooke stood up and paced to the glass doors and stood staring out.

He waited, heart thumping.

Finally, she turned around and came back, but she didn't sit down.

Not a good look, from his perspective.

'Danny, I understand your reticence over telling me all this. You're afraid to be used again. Fair enough. But the fact that you didn't trust me enough to tell me some of this is a game changer. I won't be treated like that again, by anyone. Not even you.' She spun away, looking outside again, before turning back slowly. 'I thought we were getting on especially well.' Sadness lined her words and his heart sank further.

He had failed her. But he wasn't giving up that quickly.

'We are. I care a lot for you, Brooke.' Actually, he loved her.

'Yet you continued to hold out on me. Surely when I told you how Brad used to hide deals from me until he had to come clean so I could figure a way to pay the loans you must've seen how your reticence would hurt me? How he lied to me. It hurt—a lot. So much I walked away from our relationship, and that was not something I did lightly. I'd vowed to be there through thick and thin, good times and the bad. But when I'm being used, lied to and treated as though I don't deserve the truth, then I'm out.'

'Brooke.' His heart had gone into overdrive. She couldn't leave him. They needed to talk some more. 'I made a mistake because I was afraid. I would never lie to you about anything else. I promise.'

'I'm sure you mean that, but I'm struggling to accept it. You did lie to me. It's just as bad when you do it by omission. I have learnt to protect myself, yet I still talked to you about my past in the hope you'd reciprocate. I knew you were holding something back and I tried to be patient. Where did that get me? Nowhere. It was early days, but starting a new relationship means getting to know the other person. I came to you tonight, not the other way round.' Her back was straight again, her hands tight, and a solitary tear trailed down her cheek.

Brooke was going, getting out of his life, taking his heart with her. How to prevent this? He'd said everything he could think of. Except lay his heart in her hands. Looking at her, he choked on the words *I love you*. She wasn't ready to hear them, might never be. Deep inside he could feel her need to walk away, her longing to be strong and look out for herself. If only she could understand he'd do that for her, for ever.

'I'm here for you.'

'Goodnight, Danny. I'll see you around.'

At least she had called him Danny.

CHAPTER NINE

BROOKE SAT IN the car, unable to drive with tears filling her eyes and streaming down her face. Danny hadn't been honest with her. She might have read it all, but hearing Danny put it into words—his words—made it more real, more true. It also underlined his dishonesty by omission. He'd been hiding who he really was. Sure, with good reason, but he must've known he couldn't get away with it.

Wrong, Brooke.

He hadn't hidden his kindness or generosity. Nor how he had listened to her and supported her. He was a good guy. He was also made to be a doctor. He had a firm but compassionate approach to his patients that went over very well most of the time. No one could please everyone all the time, but he came close. None of that meant he could get away with how he'd treated her. None of it.

What about the fact he'd been a famous

golfer and a hero for saving the young boy? That only made him more interesting. Did it though? Why not tell her? He must've known it would come out sooner or later. It always did, he'd said. Why risk her finding out from another source and feeling let down—as she was feeling right now? She'd have heard him out and carried on as normal, not felt so devastated. She'd have loved him more, not less.

I was falling in love with you, Danny. Truly, I was already there. You're in my heart, and my head. I get so much from being with you, I didn't want to lose that.

But now she had. Their relationship was over, gone before it had really got up to speed. She couldn't countenance Danny not owning up to his past sooner. She got why he hadn't during the first weekend they'd spent together. At the time neither of them knew how it would pan out. It might have been a weekend fling so his reticence was natural. But they'd carried on when she'd returned to Nelson. He'd had opportunities to talk to her.

She knew how this went, having learnt the hard way to be super-cautious when anyone hid something from her.

Damn you, Daniel Collins. We had something good going.

A car with a radio station's logo screeched

into the parking space in front of her and two people leapt out. The woman held a microphone and camera, the man had a pen and pad in his hand. They charged up to the apartment entrance and read the residents' names. They were out of luck if they were looking for Danny. Was that their purpose? The truth had come to light yesterday, so it was likely. Obviously the reporters were trying every apartment, pushing buttons and leaning in to speak.

So this was what Danny had to put up with. It would drive her crazy. From what he'd said, he felt the same. He no longer wanted to be the focus of bored reporters and TV viewers. Would he come down to talk to them? She doubted it.

Brooke picked up her phone, pressed a number.

'Brooke? Are you all right?'

'Danny, don't open your door. There are two reporters trying to find you by pressing every button on the board.'

'Great. And thanks. This is part of what I've been trying to keep from you.'

Only one part. How she'd have handled it was anyone's guess, but she would have stuck by him, and not looked like she was there for what she could get.

'Goodnight, Danny.' Stabbing the ignition

button, Brooke swiped a hand over her eyes, flicked on the windscreen wipers and leaned forward to see through the moisture stinging her eyes as she made her way home. Her safe place.

The house felt cold and lonely when she stepped inside and locked the door behind her. Danny had left his mark already. The couch in front of the fire where he liked to sprawl while she prepared something to eat after a difficult day at work. The cups and plates stacked in different places in the cupboard to where she'd always kept them. In her bedroom, she stared at her big bed, too big now that Danny wasn't here to share it with her and wouldn't be again. She used to love her bed. It was warm and cosy, not too hard when she went to sleep, her favourite place to read a book. The place she'd had the best sex she could remember.

She needed to forget that.

Opening a drawer in her dresser, she dug deep for a pair of fluffy pyjamas. Ugly but cosy, she didn't wear them in front of Danny, but today she needed the comfort they brought. Along with a mug of hot tea in bed, while she tried to read the thriller she'd started two days ago, because sleep wasn't going to happen any time soon, despite being exhausted after a busy shift on the ambulance and all the grief eating at her heart.

When Brooke gave up on the book after re-reading the same page four times, she turned off the light and snuggled down on her side facing where Danny had lain the other morning after they'd been to breakfast. Picking up his pillow, she breathed in the smell of him. Hugging the pillow tight to her breasts, she took more deep breaths.

How could you do this to us?

Tossing the pillow aside, she flipped onto her back and stared at the darkened ceiling. Should she forgive him and take another chance? He did appear genuinely upset he'd hurt her.

So had her mother, and her exes. Then they did it again. She had to protect her heart. No one else could. Or would.

Oh, Danny. Why, why, why?

Tears flowed again. Her eyes were going to look awful when she turned up for work. Puffy and probably still red. Not that she cared. She'd say she had a touch of flu and hopefully be sent home, away from ED and any chance of bumping into Danny if he was called in to cover for someone.

Seriously? Pull your big girl pants on and go to sleep.

Just like that? Sure thing. She did have soft,

comfy pants on, though they didn't make her feel like a tough warrior. She was exhausted, but the tears weren't abating. Yet. Give it a few minutes, and hopefully the salt water would run out.

The ringing of her phone woke her. The caller ID shocked her. So did the time. Six-thirty.

Grabbing the phone as she leapt out of bed, she answered, 'Pete, I'm sorry. I've overslept.' She never, ever did that. 'I'll be there ASAP.'

'Glad to hear. Thought you might be sick. See you shortly.'

Click.

'Guess you don't want to waste time chatting.'

Brooke dropped the phone on the bed and headed for the bathroom, trying to ignore the pounding going on in her head. Hard to believe she had slept at all, let alone through the whole afternoon. Even harder to believe she had managed to fall asleep with all the hurt and thoughts about Danny and what they'd lost going on in her head.

'Here, get that into you.'

Pam, her crew mate for the night, handed her a covered paper mug of hot coffee the moment she raced into the station. Thank goodness it wasn't Corina.

'We've got a call. I'll drive while you down the caffeine fix.'

'You're a champ. I need this more than anything else.' She sipped the coffee and winced as it burned her lip. 'That's fresh.'

'Just made it. Come on. I've checked over the ambulance, restocked and we're good to go.'

'I'm really sorry I'm late.' Was she going to spend all night apologising to people for one thing or another?

'Brooke, cut it out. You've done the same for me. It happens, okay?'

Not to me, it doesn't.

She'd start setting the alarm as backup to her errant brain from now on. 'What've we got?'

'Little old lady—eighty-three—found lying on the floor of her bedroom. She's lucid but complaining of hip pain and a sore arm.'

'Ouch. Let's hope the hip's not fractured.'

'Don't like the odds.'

'Me either.' Brooke sipped her coffee, not burning herself this time. 'Just what the doctor ordered. Thanks, again.'

'Talking of doctors—did you realise who Dr Danny really is?' Pam asked.

Here we go.

'I heard.'

'Seems Corina has been making a fool of

herself around him. But that's Corina for you. Danny's probably used to it.'

'Most likely.' Definitely. Deep in her heart she felt a twinge of sympathy for him. There would never be any getting away from what he used to do, and how famous he'd become because of it. But he took the good side, so he had to accept the other side too. Thankfully Danny had the weekend off so there was no chance of running into him. But that wasn't going to last. He did work in ED, which was also the destination of the patients they picked up.

'Joseph White, twenty-two, head knock in a rugby tackle. Lost consciousness for about five minutes,' Brooke said, looking stunned as she filled Danny in about the man she and Pam had brought into the department towards the end of her shift.

Of course he wasn't supposed to be working this weekend but, like ambulance crews, there were often staff shortages in the ED.

'Any other injuries?' he asked, trying not to stand there drinking in the sight of Brooke. It hadn't been twenty-four hours since she'd walked out of his apartment, yet it felt as if he hadn't seen her for weeks. Looking wicked in her fitted uniform, he could only think about the woman underneath the thick fabric, and not touch her or look as though he wanted to race her away and make up to her for his foolishness.

'Not that we could ascertain. We put the neck brace on in case there's been some spinal damage when Joseph was taken down by two players.' Tension tightened her slight body. She was not comfortable with him.

'That was wise. Rugby tackles are hard on the players' bodies.' He had really blown it with Brooke. Instead of getting excited about who he was, she was staying away, not trying to gain anything more than he'd already offered, and even that wasn't wanted any longer.

He looked around, found Sarah had joined them. 'Sarah, did you hear Brooke?'

'Yes, I did.' She took the notes from Brooke. 'Has anyone been notified Joseph's with us?'

'The coach was calling his partner when we left,' Brooke informed them. 'Let's transfer him and we'll get out of your way.'

Away from me, Danny thought, as they moved Joseph to the bed on the count of three. Talking to Brooke yesterday hadn't gone anywhere near as well as he'd hoped for. It had been so different to any reaction he'd had from people, especially women, that he'd been stunned. Though not surprised. Brooke had always been honest with him and had never shown any interest in him other than who he was now. His lifestyle was very wealthy, but when he'd mentioned it she'd hardly blinked. There'd certainly not been any sign of avarice lighting up her face or putting hope in her gaze.

'Anything else you need to know?' the woman who'd given him a sleepless night asked politely.

Quickly dumping the worry, he looked from Joseph to the notes Sarah held out and scanned them. 'Looks like everything I need is here.'

'Right, we're off.' Brooke was already pushing the stretcher trolley towards the ambulance bay, her shoulders tighter than usual, back straighter than straight.

His heart plummeted. Well, it would have if it hadn't already been as low as it could go.

I love you, Brooke. I know I've blown it, but can we talk?

'Do you want Joseph to have a CT scan?' Sarah brought him back to what he should be focused on.

'I'll arrange it once I've given him a complete examination. Joseph, can you hear me?'

'Yeah, man. My head hurts like stink. Those guys gave me the roughest tackle ever.'

His speech was clear and his mind was lucid, as Brooke had said.

'All part of the game, eh?'

'Yeah. Prefer it when I do the tackles, not the other way round.'

'You lost consciousness for a few minutes, so we're going to send you to Radiology for a scan. Are you hurting anywhere else?' The neck was Danny's concern, but he wasn't about to say so and give Joseph the idea. If he was in pain, he'd say so. Then again, rugby players didn't like to admit to pain very often.

'All good,' Joseph replied. 'Don't like that thing you've got around my neck. It's awkward.'

'We'll remove it soon.'

'Cheers, man.'

'You've got off lightly,' Danny told Joseph an hour later. 'But no playing rugby for at least ten days. Go back to your GP then for a clearance. Okay?'

'No.' Joseph grinned. 'I hear you. I'll behave 'cos I've got a trial with a team in Auckland next month. Missing that would be the pits.'

'I like your attitude. Good luck with the tryout.' He remembered those occasions when he'd be hyped up to do better than his best, and terrified he'd play golf like a five-year-old. Winning or getting accepted by a new coach or being included in a greater team was always the goal. 'I'll watch out to see how you do.' He'd probably just added to the man's tension.

'Thanks, Doc.'

Danny filed his report and glanced at his watch. Five forty-five. Brooke would be finishing for the day in a quarter of an hour. Chances of seeing her again today were unlikely. Unless he rang and asked if he could visit after his shift ended. But that would be late, and she had looked beat when he'd seen her earlier. Despite holding herself tall and proud, her feet had dragged when she'd been focused on the patient and not on avoiding him.

Best leave her alone, give her space so she could think about everything. Who knew? He might get a second chance.

Dreams were free.

'Want another game of golf at the weekend?' Jackson had appeared out of nowhere. 'Troy's keen to knock your socks off.'

Danny managed to laugh. This man was befriending him and hadn't once mentioned the past. 'Bring it on. What time are we booked to play?'

Another week, another payslip.

Whoop-de-doo. Exciting. Not.

Brooke threw her keys on the table and opened the fridge to get the bottle of wine she'd been into for the last couple of days. Every day had dragged since Danny's revelations. The days or nights she'd been on shift had been lacking the thrill that usually came with helping people in scary situations.

The fact was, she missed Danny. In every way imaginable. Talking on the phone late at night when they were in their own beds, sharing a meal here or in the back of a restaurant or pub, making love. It wasn't even the same seeing him in the emergency department any more. Danny was as friendly as ever, which made her uncomfortable as she tried to keep her distance, protect her heart.

It seemed all the staff now knew who they were working with, and there'd been quite a buzz for a couple of days, but it had died down pretty quickly. Corina had kept pressing Danny for attention, and no doubt a date, but she hadn't succeeded in getting even a smile. Now she was busy telling anyone who'd listen what an arrogant man he was. Brooke didn't bother telling her how wrong she was.

Flicking the igniter against a fire starter, she watched as the flames caught on the wood she'd set that morning. Winter was beginning to slip away into spring but the nights were still chilly. Especially so now that Danny wasn't around to cuddle up to or share the air with.

What if she was being unreasonable by not accepting his explanation and apology for being afraid to spoil what they had going? Had she been unfair? Possibly. But instinct was hard to ignore, and these days her instinct with relationships was to protect herself. Which could mean she'd never have another serious one, might never marry a man she loved beyond reason or have those children she'd dearly love one day. Over the years since she'd become single again she'd accepted that she mightn't have either of those, and had carried on with the things she could control. Work, home, friends. Now it wasn't enough. Because of Danny.

If she'd understood him correctly, he was missing out on the same needs too. And he seemed to want to try to have that with her, or to find out if they were compatible on all fronts at least. Had she let him down by not giving him a chance? All because he'd pushed her caution button.

Ding-dong.

'Who's that?' She didn't usually get unexpected visitors on a weeknight. Putting down her glass, she headed for the door and swung it open. Her head spun and her heart flipped. 'Danny.'

'Brooke, mind if I come in?'

Not at all. 'I suppose.' She held the door wide, shut it firmly after him. It was tempting to lock it so he couldn't walk out again. Hang on. She'd walked away from him because he'd lied to her and broken her heart along the way. 'Can I get you something to drink?' Why bother? He wasn't staying long, she'd make certain of that. He didn't belong with her any more.

'Whisky'd be great.' He seemed surprised she'd offered, as though he'd expected to be tossed out within seconds of hearing why he was here.

Why was he here? Her hand shook as she poured the whisky into the glass.

'Easy,' he said and took the bottle from her.

There was no getting away with how she felt about him being here. Nervous was one word for it. The one she hoped Danny came up with and didn't realise she was also angry at him for turning up unannounced.

His smile was bleak. Was he struggling too?

'Let's sit by the fire.' Hopefully they'd both feel a little more at ease. 'If it's still going. I'd just started it when you rang the bell.' Sure enough, the flames had died to a glow. Using the metal bar, she prodded the pieces of wood and started some small flames. 'I'll leave the firebox door open until it starts blazing.'

'Here.' Danny handed over the wine she'd

left on the bench in her hurry to move away from the tension.

Sinking into her seat, she tucked her legs underneath her butt and sipped the wine. 'How was your day?' She hadn't seen him in the ED.

'Day off. I walked up to the Centre of New Zealand and along the hills to Atawhai, did a lot of thinking.' He sipped his whisky and put the glass aside. 'I miss you, Brooke.'

Her heart banged against her ribs. Wine sloshed over the rim of her glass before she put it down too. 'I—'

I can't give in without learning more.

But how she wanted to.

'Maybe you do, Danny, but I can't forget what you did that easily.'

He winced. 'Hear me out before you say anything else.' Settling onto the couch where she had those wonderful memories of him stretched full length, sometimes nodding off for a few minutes, he twisted his glass back and forth in his fingers.

Unfair advantage, she thought as she waited for him to get to the real reason he'd come here.

'I know I should've told you who I am right from the get-go but, like I said, I enjoyed spending that weekend with you and being able to pretend none of it mattered, that you didn't need to know for that short time. Then, when we carried on seeing each other, I sort of got swept away with the normalcy of it all, not having to watch you for trouble, pretending to be like any other guy you might have dated. I felt so free, even when I knew it couldn't last and that one day someone was going to recognise me and it would all blow up in my face.' He paused, regarded her as though looking for understanding.

'The perfect reason for explaining everything to me, I'd have thought.'

'True.' He sipped his drink. 'I was playing with fire.'

'I understand to a point. But you'd found a woman who had issues about having info withheld from her, and you still didn't think to come clean.'

'It made me feel guilty more than anything else. I know how dealing with what other people have thrown at you in the past has made you jittery about revealing yourself. Yet you did tell me, and I still hung on for a few more days because I was so relaxed and happy with you.'

What else would he do that about? Brooke wondered as she tried to sip her wine without spilling any.

'What else should I have known that could've affected our relationship?'

'Like I told you, my partner, Iris, loved the money and, even more, the adulation. When the lights went out, so to speak, she wasn't as keen on being with me. I was still sought out by the media, but I wasn't heading for bigger and better things in the golfing world. I chose to step away, not linger on the periphery as a mentor or coach. No more cameras in my face, or so I thought. I know I'm repeating what I told you last week, but what I didn't say was how much it hurt. I had loved Iris for who she was, accepted everything about her. She was kind, loved kids and would go out of her way to help other people. But she changed, as I did.'

Brooke sat and waited for him to go on. She didn't want to interrupt and send him off on a tangent.

'My next relationship was short-lived for much the same reasons. That woman was more interested in living in the best house, having a top-of-the-range car, buying clothes for every time she went out the front door. She wasn't into me for me after she found out more about me. She made me cautious, which I should have learned by then. But I'd been thinking, hoping, Iris was a one-off and the next woman would see past the glamour to the real me. I've dated sporadically ever since, until I met you.' He reached for his glass, took a mouthful of whisky and set it aside again. 'You answered my dreams. You saw me for me, and I didn't want that to stop.'

'It didn't have to. I didn't know you for who you really are.'

'I know, but I didn't want to risk it.' He sighed. 'Nothing ventured, nothing gained. Only it was wonderful being so at ease with you, and I've had some hard knocks so I kind of believed there'd be another one coming. When you told me how Brad had kept important issues from you I nearly blurted it all out then, but caution won out and I shut up.'

'Come on, Danny, get real. Like you said, it was always going to come out.' Brooke studied the man in front of her. The man she'd started falling in love with one stormy weekend down in the Sounds. He was everything she'd dreamed the man in her life would be, and more. But how well did she know him? She could no longer just dive in and take a chance. She couldn't forget the lessons she'd learnt in case she got to have the life she longed for. The reality was she could very easily end up heartbroken again. 'Is there anything else you should be telling me, Danny?'

'Not about the past, no.' He took a deep

breath. 'I was going to suggest we date some more, see how it works out. People are starting to find out about me and you might not like the consequences.'

'But?'

Taking another deep breath, he looked straight at her. 'Brooke, I love you.'

'Brooke, I love you.'

The words spun through her head, filled her with hope and happiness and relief. Brought tears to her eyes. Danny loved her. She loved Danny.

He hadn't finished. 'Are you willing to take a chance on me? On the crazy things that occur because of my past? They can be annoying at best, infuriating at worst, but I'll do whatever it takes to save you from the worst.'

Wine splashed over her thighs. 'Danny, how do I know I can trust you?'

'I swear I'll never hide anything from you again. I promise.'

Easy to say.

'How can you know that? Nothing's ever that straightforward.'

The eyes that met hers were laden with sadness, and love. 'I mean it. I'll do anything in my power to be open with you about everything. There's nothing else I can say.'

She had to accept that. There was nothing more to be done at the moment about that. But her heart was shaky, and her head spinning. He said he loved her. She believed him. Did she trust him to love her for ever? To always have her back?

'What do you want for your future, Danny?'

'You. And a family, if you're willing. A home that we create together. I don't care where I live as long as it's with you.'

'You could live here in Nelson?' She wouldn't mind moving but she was testing him.

'I certainly could. It's a great place.' He gave her a hesitant smile.

Brooke nearly choked over her wine. She couldn't go on asking him questions when her heart was filling with the love she had for Danny. He was everything she'd been looking for. Everything and more. Despite what he'd done, she knew he wouldn't do it again.

She stood up on shaky legs and moved towards him. 'Danny. I love you too.' She couldn't go on. She was so overwhelmed. She'd been hurt because he hadn't talked to her about what mattered and made her think he was like other people who'd hurt her. But he loved her, and had finally told her what was important when he'd been afraid of the consequences too. This wasn't all about only her.

'You'd take a chance on me?'

'There's no taking a chance. I'm in. For everything that gets thrown at us. For all the love and fun and pain. It will be an adventure.'

Danny was standing in front of her, reaching for her hands. 'I still struggle to believe how lucky I was to meet you that day. You are awesome, Brooke. I can't explain how much I love you.' Then he was kissing her, not letting her tell him again how much he meant to her.

She leaned into his body, absorbed his strength and gentleness, drank in his kiss, felt his love in his touch, in the air around them. She kissed him back with everything she had. No doubts. No what-ifs. Just her love. They'd already wasted too much time.

Then Danny pulled back, his hands on her hips as he looked at her very seriously. Her heart thumped. What was wrong? She held her breath.

'Brooke Williams, will you do me the honour of becoming my wife?'

A smile expanded across her face. Marry Danny? 'Yes, yes, yes.'

'You're not giving in too quickly?' he asked with a cautious grin.

'Of course I am.' Brooke paused, fought the need to fling herself into his arms and get back to kissing him senseless. 'I was hurt by you not talking to me until someone else told me who you were. But—' She tapped his mouth with her finger. 'I've also been too wrapped up in my own concerns over getting hurt that I didn't really accept that you had similar concerns about being accepted for yourself.'

No caution in that grin now. It was wide and genuine and full of love. For her.

'I'll tell you something else. I've already started making enquiries about positions in emergency departments in the district.'

'You're going to specialise in emergency medicine? Not radiology?'

'You were right. I love the work I do. Why would I want to hide behind a computer screen all day? I've also had a couple of games of golf with two guys from the hospital. One of them approached me suggesting I might like to join them, obviously knowing who I was but not making any big deal out of it.'

'So you've started to get out amongst it?' Her heart was thumping. This was good for Danny, and maybe the benefits would rub off on her too, making him more relaxed whenever he went out. 'You do need to stop and settle in one place, make some lifelong friends.'

'Yes, Brooke.' He laughed. It was a sound that warmed her from top to toe. He was happy. So was she. More than happy. 'We have a lot to look forward to.' He took her hand. 'Starting right now.' His kiss was soft.

And then it wasn't. It was demanding and enticing and had to be followed up on. Brooke didn't stop kissing him back as she tugged her fiancé down to her bedroom.

* * * * *

If you enjoyed this story, check out these other great reads from Sue MacKay

Fling with Her Long-Lost Surgeon
Their Second Chance in ER
From Best Friend to I Do?
A Single Dad to Rescue Her

All available now!